Aisling Ltd

Seán Harnett worked for five years in the
IT industry in Dublin and Galway. He
currently lives in Athenry, Co. Galway.
This is his first novel.

Seán Harnett

Aisling Ltd

First published 2005 by
HAG'S HEAD PRESS
117 Capel Street
Dublin 1, Ireland
www.hagsheadpress.com

10 9 8 7 6 5 4 3 2 1

ISBN   0 9551264 0 1
ISBN-13   978 0 9551264 0 6

Printed in England by MPG Books, Bodmin, Cornwall

For Mum

Contents

0. Mission Statement

Character ... is formed primarily by a
person's work.

E.F. Schumacher

We're here to make a dent in the universe—
a new consciousness!

Steve Jobs

Why should I seek for love or study it?
It is of God and passes human wit.
I study hatred with great diligence,
For that's a passion in my own control ...

W.B. Yeats

1. Executive Summary

Larry was always telling me that my writing needed to be more concise, that I shouldn't go on so much, that I ought to learn to bullet point information. *We're living in a time of accumulating information*, he'd say, *nobody has time to sift through everything*— so that's why I'm just going to tell you straight out what happened, without messing you around. A gang of us from work went fishing for shark, and I killed him, I killed Larry.

How's that for getting to the point?

*

It is the morning of the last Sunday in July, 2000. I am leaning over the side of the *Maeldun*, an old trawler turned charter-fishing boat out of Castletownbere, watching the sea slice itself open on the bow of the boat. The bisected waves sloop under the hull, and I count them as they lift and drop and lift and drop us again, one two three, four five six. I count to ward off the nausea I am feeling, but it isn't doing anything for me. I had also, as we'd cleared the harbour, inserted a swab of cotton into my left ear canal and fixed my attention on the horizon that opened out before us, south-south-west between the headlands of Bantry Bay. I gather that this will preserve my body's equilibrium, but it isn't working either: each up and down and up and down again and up and down and up and down again motion of the boat is matched by a contraction and loosening of the muscles of my stomach, as if an invisible hand is squeezing it steadily.

I lose my count and begin again, one two three, better than doing nothing, four five six, trying to match my breathing with the rhythm of the rollers, in and out and in again, trying to keep my body distracted from the queasiness, seven eight nine.

The excursion is Larry's idea. It's not the first time I've been on a trip like this with him. Since joining Aisling Ltd I've had to endure a lot of different kinds of Boys' Own shite: hill-walking, orienteering, mountain-biking, kayaking, those corporate team-building exercises in which you have to build a raft from a few planks, a length of rope and some leaky barrels—all that kind of stuff. Today's excursion is thankfully more of a perk than a team-building exercise. The gossip in the guest-house last night was that Larry had read in one of his CEO magazines that shark-fishing was *the* new executive activity and that's why, to celebrate the signing of the Ninth Wave deal, he had brought the Project Team away to the Beara for the weekend, with the optional extra of a day's fishing on the Sunday.

I look to where he stands not far from me, leaning casually against the gunwale. He is wearing a Breton fisherman's hat and brand new oilers, which reach to his midriff and are held up at the waist by two braces that loop from behind each shoulder to form parallel lines down the front of his spotless white Aran sweater. He seems too much the part—Larry the Fisherman, with a big fat fucking capital-F—but then he always manages to arrogate the Proper Noun for whatever activity he engages in— Larry the Hill-Walker, Larry the Rock-Climber, Larry the Canoeist—as if a pioneer in everything he does.

He catches me appraising him.

'Isn't this just the business?' he shouts, throwing the words to me over the grinding clatter of the engine.

'It would be,' I shout back, 'if I didn't feel so sick.'

'Fix your eyes on the horizon, like James told you.'

'I have. I am. It doesn't seem to work.'

'How can you be sick on such a beautiful day?' he asks. 'Just breathe that air.' He extends his arms before him like a sorcerer invoking the elements, snorting the wind into his lungs. 'Wonderful. Just fucking wonderful. Better than any drug.'

It is not the first time that I've heard Larry employ the Anglo-Saxon, so it can't be shock that causes the delicate balance I have achieved to tip over, but tip it does. My stomach heaves. I drain into the sea a spume of vomit that's tossed up into a foaming cluster of bubbles. It reminds me of cuckoo-spit.

'Bit early for the rubby dubby, mate,' says James from the wheelhouse. James is our skipper. He's Australian.

'Rubby dubby?' I ask, wiping my mouth with the cuff of my old fleece sweater.

'Chum,' replies James. 'Burley. Bait.'

'For the sharks?'

'Of course for the sharks. They're not goin to come visiting for the company, are they mate? We have to make sure that we give em a decent feed.'

'What's in it?'

'I don't think I should tell you if you're feelin a bit dodge.'

'Fish?' asks Larry.

'Ground up fish,' says James with relish. 'Blood, guts, bones, scales—the whole fuckin jar of Marmite.'

'Don't,' I plead, but my stomach heaves again; all that is dredged up this time is a slick of bile that coats the back of my throat with an acidic tang.

'When will we be laying out?' asks Larry. I suppose 'laying out' is a technical term and wonder where he picked it up.

'Soon, mate,' says James. 'A few more miles and we'll be right.'

'And then what happens?'

'Then we fish.'

'For blue shark?'

'Yes, for blue shark.'

'How many are we likely to catch?'

'Jesus, mate, I don't know. On a good day we might get ten or twenty of the buggers. On a bad day we might get none.'

'And will this be a good day?'

'I can't guarantee anything, mate.'

'Not even for the money we're paying?'

'It's in the contract you signed, mate: there are absolutely no guarantees on the ocean, no matter how much money you have. First law of the sea.'

A few minutes later James cuts the engine and releases the anchor. We have strayed out of sight of land and are enclosed now all around by a diadem of horizon. Eastwards the horizon is clear, but a herd of clouds waddles towards us from the west; they trail thick, dark columns of rain.

James casts his eyes in the direction of the rain and stands considering it. Larry notices.

'Is that bad news?'

'The weather forecast said we should be right,' says James. He claps his hands together and rubs his palms. 'Okay, time to put somethin in the water that the sharks will appreciate.' He moves back into the wheelhouse and emerges a few moments later with a battered catering-sized container, which might once have contained coffee, cradled in his arms. He hands it to Brendan, head of the Ninth Wave Project Team. Brendan's new to Aisling, a business analyst who joined the company after Tom Drover's mutiny. I hardly know him. He has just stood up from being sick over the side of the boat. 'Here, hold this.'

Brendan takes the tin. James strides back into the wheel-house.

Brendan hefts the tin up and down in his arms. 'Cold,' he says.

'That's cause it's just out of the fridge,' says James, treading back onto the deck. He holds a hammer and a large flathead screwdriver, and carries a small plastic crate under his left arm. He gets Brendan to set the tin down onto the deck and then pries the lid off the container with the flathead. An aroma is released that smells of rancid cod liver oil, loam turned during a dirty spring, the inside of a freezer in need of a defrost, damp corn flakes, and the most distant intimation of freeze-dried caffeine.

'Is that the rubby dubby?' asks Larry.

'Sure is.'

'Did you make it yourself?'

James laughs. 'Shit, mate,' he says, 'I'd love to tell you that this is my own secret recipe but, nah, I buy it from the bait shop in Castletown. Makin this stuff yourself can really stink up your house and the missus wouldn't be too happy with that.'

He has jammed the crate over the lidless end of the tin, and is now securing the two together with bungee cords. 'Got this idea off the Web,' he explains. 'Before, I used to just put the chum tin into a nylon diver's bag and hang that over the end of the boat, but the tin would always sink and sometimes a shark would get entangled in the mesh of the bag and I'd have to drag it on board, try to untangle it and get it back into the water before it bit my bloody fingers off.'

'I remember that,' says Basking.

'Remember what, Paddy?' asks James. He is attaching rigid plastic floats to the crate.

'I remember when that happened.'

'It happened more than once, Paddy, but yeah, you were there when it happened one time.'

Padraig 'Basking' Finn is Aisling Ltd's CFO. His input into the Ninth Wave project had been minimal, but he owned a holiday home in the area and knew James and had gotten us a special rate. I hadn't known that he'd been out with James before, though.

'Well it was my first time out with you,' says Basking, graciously accepting James's mild rebuke, 'and it was very memorable.'

'They're all a blur to me,' says James. He attaches a nylon line to the crate and dumps it over the stern. It bobs woozily in the water, like an inflatable punch bag struggling to regain its stability after being slugged.

'Should it be doing that?' asks Larry.

'Doin what?'

'Just bobbing there. Shouldn't it be going further out behind us?'

'The line will extend itself once we start driftin.'

'Drifting?'

'Sure, Larry,' says Basking, cutting in before James, who has begun to sound bored with Larry's questions, can answer. 'As soon as James has set up the rods, he'll raise the anchor, and we'll start drifting back to shore.'

'I see,' says Larry.

James begins to assemble the rods and the lines. The others are not interested. They look out to sea, or hang over the side of the boat to get sick. Basking reads a newspaper. Larry watches what James does and I watch with him.

James is aware of Larry's interest and seems resigned to explaining to us what he's doing. But Larry is not a good listener. He keeps interrupting to ask questions. Why three rods? he enquires. What kind of rods are these? What are you using for bait? How deep will the lines go? What's this? What's that?

James manages to work despite Larry's queries. Soon three large black rods stand in holders on the stern gunwale, angled out over the water, their lines intersecting the swell at different distances from the boat. James pops into the wheelhouse again, and then quickly pops back out. I hear the grinding of the anchor being raised. The boat begins to move slowly, and the lines stiffen.

'What now?' asks Larry.

'Now we wait,' says James, 'and drink tea.'

*

Draughts of tepid tea and coffee are dispensed from two large flasks into enamelled mugs gnarled by years of use.

'Is there no drink on this boat?' asks Basking.

'Not a chance,' says James. 'If one of you fools got drunk and fell overboard I'd be sued for so much my grandchildren would still be payin off the debt.'

Basking reaches inside his jacket and pulls out a small, slim, silver-plated flask. 'What if one of us fools had brought the drink on board himself?'

'Christ, Paddy, you'll put me out of business.'

'Relax, James, it's just a wee drop. Warm the cockles, you know; take the nip out of the air.' He passes among the group, pouring a dram of piss-gold liquid into all our cups, including mine (which surprises me, though I notice that I am given less than the others). He comes to James. 'You want some?'

'What the fuck,' he says. 'No cops out here to breathalyse me.'

'That's the spirit.' Basking holds up the flask and shakes it from side to side. 'You fancy a tot, Larry?'

'I'm not a big fan of spirits; you know that, Padraig.'

'I think you should make an exception for this: it's a very special single still malt from the Whisky Club in Edinburgh.'

'That's OK, Padraig.'

'Suit yourself,' says Basking as he tips the dregs of the whisky in the flask into his cup. 'Anyone know any sea shanties?'

No one says anything.

'James?'

James shakes his head.

'Jesus. What kind of sailors are we if we don't know any songs of the sea?'

'No one sings shanties any more, Paddy,' says James. 'Or if they do they sing them in Cantonese or Bangladeshi, not English.'

'Another lost tradition.' Basking sighs with mock despair. He clears his throat. 'Here's one I think everyone will know,' he says and begins to sing in an out-of-tune bass:

Oh show me the way to go home

Brendan laughs and joins in:

I'm tired and I wanna go to bed

We all sing along now, except Larry:

I had a little drink about an hour ago
And it's gone right to my head

'I don't get it,' says Larry, when we stop to draw breath before the next verse.

'It's from *Jaws*,' I explain. 'From the scene when the three guys are on the boat at night, waiting for the shark to attack.'

'Just before the shark attacks the boat for the first time,' says Brian, a systems architect and technical consultant to the Ninth Wave Project Team.

'I've never seen *Jaws*,' says Larry.

'How can you never have seen *Jaws*?' asks Basking. 'It's on television the whole fucking time.'

'I don't watch much television.'

'There's no chance of a shark attacking us out here, is there?' asks Brendan.

'None whatsoever, mate,' says James. 'There isn't a shark large enough or pissed off enough in the Atlantic to attack a boat.'

'A boat this size,' interjects Basking.

'Well, sure,' says James. 'If you were in a life-raft or a rowin boat you might have some cause for concern.'

I turn away from the conversation. Taking the whisky in my tea was perhaps a bad idea: my nauseated stomach, which had calmed itself when the boat was at anchor, has begun to slosh around inside me again and caustic bubbles of air burst in my throat. I turn my gaze to the horizon to steady myself. Something moves in my peripheral vision.

'Hey,' I say, 'I think one of the rods just twitched.'

Everyone turns to stare with me at the rods. A party balloon is attached to the line of each rod at the point where it sinks into the water. The balloon on the line farthest out is bobbing up and down like a child's bath toy. The rod twitches again, the tip bending towards the water in supplication.

'The term is "pulled",' says James quietly.

'Do we have a shark?' asks Larry.

The balloon pops and the rod bends sharply.

'We sure do,' says James, who is grinning broadly. 'That was bloody quick.'

'Auspicious day,' I suggest.

'What?'

'Perhaps it's an auspicious day for shark fishing,' says Larry slowly, as if he is speaking to someone who doesn't really understand English.

'Please yourself, mate,' says James, lifting the butt of the rod from its holder and placing it into the butt-guard attached to the harness he has strapped on. 'Now, auspicious day or not, this is how this is gonna work. I'll take the first shift and stonk this bastard out. Then whoever wants to have a go can take it in turns to reel him in. Or one person can do it all on their own. I don't care. Decide among yourselves. Now pay attention to what I'm doin. It's called pumpin.'

He explains pumping, demonstrating how one lowers and raises the rod in order to reel in the catch. I zone out his words to follow with my eyes the taut of the line as it stretches from the tip of the rod to the point where it submerges. It is not static: it moves from side to side.

'What size do you think he is, James?' asks Larry.

'Five, six feet maybe; ninety to a hundred pounds.'

'Is that big?'

'It's about average.'

'What's the biggest fish you've ever caught?'

'The biggest fish I ever landed was a marlin I snagged in the Caribbean,' he replies, then winces as he drops the rod. 'But one time I hooked this Mako on a boat out of Nantucket. Biggest fuckin fish I've ever seen.'

'Mako?'

'A short-fin Mako shark, mate. Not as famous as the Great White but a whole fuckin continent meaner. This one was easily twelve feet from snout to tail; a fully grown adult female.'

'What happened?'

'She fuckin snapped the line, didn't she? Two fuckin hours and she just snaps the hook and swims off. I think maybe she was havin some sport with me; that I was the one being played, not her. Best date I ever had, though.'

Larry acts as if he is listening, but I can tell from his expression that he already has his next question queued and has merely been waiting for a pause before asking it.

'How long do you think it will take to reel this shark in?'

It takes James a few moments to respond and when he does it's to say, 'Sorry, mate, miles away. What did you ask me?'

'I asked how long it will take to reel in this shark.'

'That depends on how much fight he has in him. I reckon

this one's a good sport, though. He'll give you your money's worth.'

'Will we each get a go on the rod?'

'If we do it right. You feel up to it now?'

'Sure,' says Larry. 'Absolutely.'

James spreads his legs so that his feet are shoulder-width apart, and angles his bum as if perching himself on an imaginary stool.

'Stand right beside me,' he instructs. Larry steps up beside him so that James is to his right. 'Stand like how I'm standin.' Larry mirrors James's body position. Now James lifts the rod out of his butt-guard and slides it into the guard strapped to Larry's waist. Larry places his hands on the rod.

'Good,' says James. 'Little higher up.'

Larry slides his hands up the rod.

'You got it?'

Larry nods.

'You sure?'

'Yes,' says Larry impatiently.

James releases his hold on the rod and steps away. Larry just stands there. 'Pump,' says James. 'Remember to pump the rod.'

Larry dips the rod, but when he tries to pull it back it seems stuck.

'Reel out a bit of line,' says James. He steps up behind Larry and guides him through the motion a couple of times, then backs off.

'How does that feel?' he asks when Larry has had unaided control of the rod for a minute or two, lifting and dropping the rod with a look of pure, childish concentration. At James's question, though, he smiles.

'Primal,' he says; 'it feels primal.'

'Of course it bloody does, mate: you've got a monster at the end of that line.'

Larry repeats the word *monster* in a whisper.

James continues to talk: 'We're doin for sport, you know, what our ancestors did for survival. Too bloody right it feels primal.'

'Our ancestors didn't have graphite rods and boats equipped with state-of-the-art GPS,' says Basking, who has moved to the stern and now stands to Larry's left.

James shrugs. 'They also didn't have to pay back a mortgage on their boats, so we're even.'

Basking doesn't offer a response and the conversation lulls. No one else speaks. We are all looking at Larry. He seems to be working hard. He grimaces each time he pulls back on the rod.

'You OK there, mate?' asks James after Larry grunts loudly following the completion of a long, hard pull-back.

'I'm fine,' he says, though his voice sounds strained.

'There's no point in stonkin yourself out, mate. We could be at this all day. There'll be plenty of fish yet.'

Larry nods, then jerks his head around to look at James. 'Something's wrong. I don't feel anything on the line anymore.'

James takes the rod from him. 'I think we've lost him,' he says. 'Must have slipped the hook.'

'What happened? What did I do wrong?'

'You did nothin wrong. These things happen. We'll rebait the line—'

'Wait,' says Basking, 'I think it's taken the second hook.'

The second rod, whose line is maybe twenty or twenty-five feet closer in to the boat, twitches. Basking takes the rod and slots it into his butt-guard. He handles the rig more confidently than Larry, makes the process look less labour-intensive.

'How's he runnin, Paddy?' asks James.

'I think he's fucking surfacing,' says Basking, yanking his gaze along the trajectory of the line to where it pierces the water and intersects with a fly-black silhouette that grows larger as it nears the surface. Maybe fifteen metres out a fin appears. I had thought that the fin of a shark would sever the waves hard and sharp, but this fin flops instead from side to side like a stubby column of jelly being dragged behind a speedboat.

'Jesus,' says James, 'this one is bloody eager.'

'Does this happen often?' asks Larry, trying not to sound disappointed, and almost succeeding.

'Not often,' says James. 'But sometimes one of them will practically jump onto the deck, almost like it wants to be caught.'

'Suicidal sharks,' suggests Larry.

'Maybe.' James does not sound convinced. But he is not giving his attention to Larry. His cocked head is aimed along the sight of Basking's line. Basking drops the rod and plays out a length of line, then lifts and reels it back in, then does this again, and again, jerking the shark a little closer with each repetition, as if he isn't fishing so much as bringing an unruly dog to heel.

Ten metres from the boat. The shark does not want to come any further. It regains its fight. It swims against the hook, its fin smacking loudly against the water, desperate, its tail thrashing behind it, slapping up spray and spume. Basking stumbles forward and almost drops the rod. James skips up behind him and grabs his harness.

'What the fuck are you doing?' asks Basking.

'Just a reflex,' says James.

'Let go of me and don't stand so fucking close.'

Five metres from the boat. James has stepped away from Basking and now stands ready with a gaff at the gate in the stern. Four three two metres. I turn away and look at Larry, who stands to Basking's left, his eyes flicking between Basking and the shark. He looks worried.

Probably a metre now.

Then Larry's expression changes. In the moment before I turn in reaction to simultaneous grunts of satisfaction from James and Basking, I read resentment in his face. Enough information for me to surmise that they have landed the shark. And, yes, when I turn, James is dragging the fish through the open stern gate while Basking is replacing the rod in its holder and stands with his arms folded, looking content but not smug.

James works efficiently to retrieve the hook, measure the long, lean, tapering body, tag it, photograph it cradled in Basking's arms and release it back into the sea as quickly as possible. I wonder how it is feeling and fancy that its blank black eye catches my own. No, not blank: don't want to suggest that it is lifeless: not that. And so delicate looking. The eye is like a bubble of oil or a dark egg yolk that might burst if you touched it. Indifferent, perhaps, but alive, very much alive, and strangely fragile despite its ferocious profile. And not even indifferent, no. For want of a better word. Uncomprehending, maybe. And incomprehensible. A different order of life certainly. Apart from us, completely removed from the human sphere.

When it is released I watch it flick away. Its head dives and the eyes with it. Its silhouette darts, darkens and disappears.

Then Larry speaks, asking, 'Will there be more sharks for us to catch?'

'Sure,' says James. 'There'll be plenty more sharks.'

*

While we wait for another shark to attack the lines, the clouds I had seen earlier come hobbling over us, dragging with them a lash of grim, insistent rain. We sit in silence with the hoods of our oilers and raincoats pulled forward over our brows. I watch the moisture gather on my brim in drops that linger, then detach and fall gravely one by one to the deck.

Everything is quiet; the world is muted. The gulls that had flown in our wake, following the chum slick, are gone. The waves are pulling their punches against the *Maeldun*'s hull. No one's really talking. And I've gone inwards, not thinking, not even really day-dreaming, just attending to the emotion that had appeared—that I'd become aware of—when Larry had asked his question of James: *Will there be more sharks for us to catch?* The yearning in his voice affected a physical reaction in me, and my consciousness is beginning at last to comprehend the changes being wrought in my body, the tightened muscles, the pulsing, pumping blood-flow in my head, the constrictions in my stomach, the prickling skin.

Hate. The feeling that has overcome me (overcome me again, I should say) is hate. Hate leading to resolution. To *a* resolution.

*

The rain passes. Hours pass. We have by now hooked and released six sharks, all small- to medium-sized. Clouds are accumulating once again in the west and the waves—relatively docile until now—have frothed up, a strong breeze driving them into whitecaps that rock the boat from right to left. We have drifted back into sight of land, and another shark has taken the hook.

It's a big one, nine or ten feet long, easily the largest bluey

James has ever seen in Irish waters—or so he claims; he could be having us on—and he insists we strap into the fighting chair at the stern before 'running the mother'. Brendan and Brian have both had their turns at reeling in the shark, and I am now persuaded to have my go. I strap myself in. I place my hands on the rod and as soon as James releases his hold, I feel a weight at the end of the line, a strong, vivid weight, swimming backwards and forwards in a loop, switching hard against the limits of the line like a caged panther.

I am struck by the emptiness of the endeavour. We have, like magicians, summoned this creature from another reality, from its realm, in order to bind it to ours. And for what purpose? We are not going to consume it. At least, not physically; we won't eat its meat, or its viscera, but I suppose we will ingest what it represents, its symbolic essence, in order to fuel our egos, and the thought that Larry of all people should be not only encouraging but participating in this fantasy ... it only confirms me in what I intend to do.

James senses my distraction and asks if I have had enough. I tell him yes, let him take the rod, and release myself from the chair. I stand up, feeling displaced. Another rush of hate—for myself, for those with me on the boat. For Larry. He has taken the rod after me but is refusing to bind himself into the chair. James is trying to pry the rod from him; Basking is mediating.

'Listen, James,' he says, 'you'll be well paid for this. We'll make sure you get a large bonus. Just let Larry do what he wants.'

'Spare me the bullshit, Paddy,' says James. 'If your mate here gets pulled over, that's me finished. I'll never be able to get insurance on the boat again.'

'We won't sue.'

'Everyone fuckin sues.'

'We won't sue,' insists Larry, struggling to maintain his balance as he pumps the rod.

James releases his hold on the rod, his arms flaying in exasperation. 'There's always some cunt who thinks he's Ernestfuckin-Hemingway,' he shouts. 'It'll serve you right if you go over, you stupid bloody Mick.'

Larry does not seem to register the insult. He totters towards the stern gunwale, rigid tendons stretching the skin in his neck. But he shrugs off Basking's hands when the bigger man tries to balance him.

'This one's mine, Padraig,' he says.

Basking stands back, hands held up.

Yes, I hate Larry: especially Larry. And even though I would love to tell you that I hate him for some terribly profound reason—for some tragic Shakespearian flaw for which the cosmos has sanctioned death, or for his actions: for what he did to Tom, for how he treated Fergus, for what happened between Deirdre and me only two days before—there really is no reason, no good reason anyway. Yet I nonetheless find myself inching across the deck towards him. I find myself putting out my hands. I find myself, as Larry is tugged forward on his toes, placing them on his back at shoulder and hip height.

I find myself pushing.

Larry flails forward. His body pivots around the gunwale at the thighs and disappears into the water.

'Blueys are not man-eaters,' James had reassured us before we'd left port, 'but they have been known to take chunks out of people in the water so make sure you don't fall in.'

James had also mentioned that the favourite colour of blue sharks is life-jacket orange and although Larry isn't wearing a life-jacket his oilers are banana-skin yellow and that's close enough I hope.

The shark is coming for Larry, who's sinking. He's splashing and kicking to stay afloat, but he's sinking. And the shark is nearly on him. It is big. Seems easily a third the length of the *Maeldun*. We can all see its cobalt-blue body bearing down on Larry, the line still hooked in its mouth, the rod dragging along behind it.

Larry can see it too, can see it steering for him, and he screams. That's right you bastard, I think: scream. Scream.

Case Study I

(Source: employment notice, *The Irish Times*, 02/07/1999)

COMMUNICATING THE STORY OF OUR BUSINESS

Every business has a story to tell.

The story of Aisling Ltd is about the unique vision and rapid growth of an Irish-based IT solutions provider to the financial, telecommunications and process manufacturing sectors.

As our Content Specialist, your job will be to make sure that this story is *heard*.

We are looking for an exceptional individual, with vast reserves of flair, creativity and passion, to take ownership of the company's brand identity and ensure that we consistently and emphatically articulate our core values and wide-ranging competencies to both existing and potential clients.

You will be responsible for managing and driving change across a diverse portfolio of communication channels, including the company website, corporate brochures, press releases, client *communiqués*, sales letters, and informational circulars.

You will also be responsible for inculcating a sense of brand stewardship within the company through a systematic programme of in-house communications and training events.

Sound like a challenge? It is! Your application will convince us that you are an original and innovative communicator (preferably with a journalistic background), with the drive and ambition to make an immediate and sustained impact on the successful dissemination of the Aisling story, both internally and externally.

In addition, you will convince us that you thrive on being regularly pushed beyond your confidence zone. You will convince us that you are open to new and revolutionary ways of doing business. You will convince us that you are a team-player *and* an individual, ready to take risks on behalf of the company. You will convince us that you have singular ideas that you want to see put into action.

In return, Aisling offers you the opportunity of working in a dynamic, future-focused environment, where the rewards are significant. The Aisling employee package includes a generous basic salary, as well as a share-option scheme, a pension scheme, health insurance, and subsidised gym membership.

Applications, including an up-to-date CV and samples of your writing, to careers@aislingltd.com.

Aisling Ltd—where 'career' is more than just a noun.

2. Origins:
The Biography of Aisling

My career with Aisling began almost exactly a year before the shark-fishing trip, on the first Monday in August, 1999.

I had intended to get up at seven that morning. This would have given me plenty of time to make the seven-forty train into town, but I was actually out of bed fifteen minutes before the alarm went off and, after showering and dressing quickly, left the house without bothering to have breakfast (couldn't have stomached the thought of it anyway) in order to catch the seven-twenty service.

Outside, the sun seemed caught on the horizon in a swaddling band of stratus, but there was a busy sky above—strips of cirrus driving easterly—and below, at sea level, a lean breeze that snapped at the hem of my jacket and skipped and scurried around the legs of the other early risers hurrying, like me, to the station. I arrived as the train was pulling in, bought my ticket and shuffled into one of the carriages. It was already crammed with passengers from Drogheda and Balbriggan. There was nowhere to sit. I had to stand to attention in the aisle, my satchel pressed to my side, mindful, as the journey progressed, of the sweat accumulating on my back and the way in which it gummed my shirt to a widening patch of skin on either side of my spine.

Grateful, then, when we slurred into Connolly just before eight, but also aware that I was early, much too early. I didn't want to appear that eager, so I found a café on Talbot Street where I ordered an espresso, then another, and one more's the trick, consuming each with gluttony sips so that the buzz would seep quickly into my system. Which it did, accumulating like a static charge behind my eyeballs, and generating a jittery energy in my stomach that surged every now and then, setting my hands and arms shaking.

I paid and left at twenty to nine, making my way past the IFSC in the direction of the Liffey. Crossing the river, I found myself in the midst of a crowd of men and women moving in the same direction as me; we were pushing through a stream of people coming from Moss Street and the southern quays, and I suddenly and unexpectedly felt as if I was part of a current that lost itself in a meeting with another, until we diverged at City Quay and flowed on in our separate directions.

This sense of the crowd as an entity or phenomenon larger

than the sum of its constituents disoriented me, and I had to stop to recover my breath, though I told myself it was nothing really, just the coffee, and the consequences of not having slept well the night before. I had in fact lain awake for most of the night, compulsively checking the clock, each time I'd picked it up thinking that surely an hour or more had passed—to find that time had clicked forward by only a few minutes. My sense of reality had become skewed; and when I had slept the dreams into which I'd flitted had been so fine and weightless and oddly literal that they were hardly dreams at all, more like visual distortions in which my room, and the furniture in it, had become fluid and unstable, as if I was looking at the world from just below the surface of a film of water. And just now, as I had been buffeted through the crowd, trying but failing to fight my immersion in the tide, I'd experienced a similar sense of detachment, and had wondered if I wasn't still asleep and dreaming all of this.

Momentarily wondered. Just the sleep deprivation, of course. And the coffee. And the fact that I was nervous.

Nervous. Oh yes, nervous.

I turned off the docks into the street in which Aisling's Dublin office was located. It was a three-storey building that had once been a granary or a hopstore, but had a few years ago been renovated to provide commercial space—as had the building beside it, the headquarters of an architectural firm, and the building across the street, a media production house.

I idled before the door for a few moments, then rang the bell. I was, after a few moments, buzzed in.

'Thanks,' I said by way of greeting to the receptionist; she sat behind a counter that was down a few steps from the entrance.

'Can I help you?' she asked in a pleasant, but formal and somewhat securocratic tone.

'I'm meant to be starting work here today,' I explained, 'joining Deirdre Heffernan's team.'

'Yes, of course,' she said, smiling. 'Eoin, isn't it? Welcome to Aisling. Deirdre is expecting you, but she's on a conference call at the moment. She asked me to tell you that she'll be down in a few minutes and to send her apologies for not being here to greet you herself.'

'That's no problem.'

'Why don't you take a seat while you're waiting?' She indicated a terracotta-coloured couch flush with the wall opposite her station. 'I'm Sheila, by the way.'

'Pleased to meet you,' I said, sitting down.

'Would you like a tea or coffee?'

'Tea'd be lovely,' I said.

I flicked through the business magazines and the daily papers that were arranged on the coffee table in front of the couch but couldn't concentrate on them. Then, as Sheila placed a cup of tea on the table, the nervousness that had been present—but largely inchoate—since I'd gotten up congealed and settled in my stomach like old fat in a fryer. I worried that it would stand against me if I threw up on my first day with the company: first impressions and all that. Closed my eyes, tried to breathe through it.

'Well hello there,' said a voice, a female voice. I opened my eyes and looked up to see Deirdre standing before me. I stood and took the hand she offered; we shook.

'You don't look so great,' she said, glancing at the untouched cup of tea in front of me.

'I must have eaten something dodgy for breakfast,' I lied.

'Nervous?'

I hesitated before I answered, wondering how it would

affect her impression of me if I was to tell the truth. 'A little,' I said, hedging my response. It was a relief to concede even this much, to articulate, however guardedly, the sensation I was experiencing.

'Well,' said Deirdre, with a smile and a tilt of the head that I assumed were meant to put me at ease, 'I don't want to make you any more nervous, but Lawrence is in the office, and I'd like you to meet him before we do anything else.'

'Fine,' I said, trying to keep my voice level, and succeeding so much that Deirdre asked, 'You do know who Lawrence is, right?'

'Of course,' I said, 'Aisling's CEO. He's become quite a celebrity.'

'Hasn't he?' said Deirdre, with something approaching pride. 'And that's why I want you to meet him right away. He's rarely in the country, let alone in the office: it's a bit of an opportunity.'

She led me up a stairway as she talked. My eyes involuntarily ranged over the view her hind presented, noting the creases in the legs of her charcoal-grey trouser suit and the long, black tapering pumps she wore (they had a slight upturn at the toes like a witch's boot), while my mind speculated whether or not she was aware that I was scrutinising her in this way, and if she was, whether or not it would bother her. Yet when we reached the second-floor landing, and she turned to check that I was still in train, she had on her the same welcoming and ingenuous face that had greeted me.

The floor was almost wholly dominated by its landing; taking up fully two-thirds of the available space, it was crammed with desks and cubicles, and a huge assembly of computers that I assumed were the office's routers and servers. The rest of it was fenced off by an MDF partition that rose from the floor to the ceiling. It was inset with Perspex panels.

'The boardroom,' said Deirdre quietly, as she opened a door in the partition and stepped aside to let me into the room beyond. A man sat inside at the far end of a long, rounded, oak-finished conference table, talking into the mouthpiece of the mobile headset dangling from his left ear. A laptop was propped open in front of him. He didn't look up as we entered but held aloft a finger to let us know that he knew we were there and would be with us in a moment.

I concentrated on taking in the details of the room (a dozen chairs around the table; a large abstract canvas on the back wall; comms sockets in the skirting; a whiteboard on which someone had been writing: 'client facing solutions', 'data subjects', 'key learnings', 'bed down'; a projector; and a three-fingered confer-ence phone that looked like a matt-plastic starfish washed up onto some faux-wooden shore) to distract myself from the details of the man's conversation, but it was difficult to filter out his bullish tone.

'And then one day we woke up and realised, bloody hell, but the country is a success, and everyone is talking about com-puters and IT and isn't it great?, and every gouger you meet has an e-commerce strategy, and foreigners are flocking to work here, and you can get decent Italian ground coffee and tinned artichoke hearts in the Spar around the corner.'

He paused to listen to what his caller had to say, then nodded his head, which set his mouthpiece shaking.

'Exactly. And why shouldn't we worship money? We've *always* worshipped money and wealth.'

He paused again.

'Yes, even in Ireland,' he went on. 'Cattle were sacred in pre-Christian Ireland, did you know that? And not because they were the sacred creatures of some god or goddess or anything like that, but because they were the bloody medium of exchange. And the Ardagh Chalice? Jesus Christ, what's that but the worship of money made manifest? And I know I shouldn't get started about the Church but you do know why the priests and bishops are so pissed off about the Celtic Tiger, don't you? Not because of some dilution of the nation's spiritual life, but because it means they are no longer the wealthiest people in Ireland. The flock is not only finally thinking for itself, but living in bigger houses and driving bigger cars, and the clergy can't fucking stand it.'

A longer pause.

'Of course it's about power. It has always been about power. Money is power. And whoever has the power is worshipped. It's like economics meets Carl Jung. Or Disney's circle-of-life grafted onto Adam bloody Smith.'

Another pause, near the end of which he began to laugh.

'Naturally I'm bullshitting you,' he said. 'Mostly bullshitting you. Listen, I have to go—there's someone here who wants a word with me. Yeah, yeah, I'll talk to you later.'

He disconnected.

'Jesus Christ, Lawrence,' said Deirdre, 'I hope that wasn't a journalist.'

'Of course not,' he said, getting up from his chair and extracting the plug from his ear. 'And even if it was a journalist, I'd only say things like that off the record. So, Dee, who do we have here?'

'This is Eoin Cullen, Lawrence,' she said. 'He's joining my team today. Eoin, this is Lawrence Cooley.'

'Eoin,' he said, 'pleased to meet you.'

'Lawrence,' I said, taking the hand he had offered me. He was wearing a turquoise silk shirt with a sunflower-yellow tie.

A navy suit jacket hung over the back of his chair. The blue slacks and green jacket I was wearing seemed suddenly dowdy.

'For the love of God call me Larry,' he said. 'No one except Deirdre calls me Lawrence. Alright?'

'Alright.'

'So,' said Larry, and paused, perhaps waiting for me to say something. I smiled at him.

'Deirdre tells me that you went to university in Dublin,' he said before the silence had become too awkward.

'That's right,' I replied, grateful that he'd said something.

'Trinity?'

'No, not Trinity,' I said slowly, made cautious by something in his tone; I was sure that this admission had cost me something, though I couldn't fathom why it should cost me anything.

'Ah, pity,' he said. 'I knew our little clique would have to come to an end eventually.'

'Lawrence,' said Deirdre, 'don't tease him. He has no idea what you're talking about.'

'I'm sorry, Eoin,' he said, 'it's just that everyone we've appointed to a senior position since we've been in business has had a degree of some sort from Trinity. I was wondering how long we could keep going before we'd exhaust Trinity's stockpile and have to start recruiting from the lesser institutions.'

'Lawrence,' said Deirdre, 'you can't say that!' She turned to me: 'He's just pulling your leg; he doesn't really mean it.'

'Of course I don't really mean it,' he said, directing his remark at Deirdre.

'You have no tact,' she said, trying to sound prim, but unable to keep herself from smiling at him.

Larry returned her smile. 'What good did tact ever do anyone?' he asked, laughing. I supposed that it must have been a private joke between them. 'And besides I have you and your team to edit me so that I sound like I'm just positively brimming over with tact. Eoin here will be my tact man, won't you Eoin?'

'I'll do my best.'

'You'll do better than that,' he stated, though there was no trace of coercion that I could detect in his voice, just a plain statement of fact. 'Look, it was a pleasure meeting you, Eoin Cullen, but I have a rake more calls to get through, so you'll have to sod off I'm afraid. And Dee, I'll talk to you later, OK?'

'Sure,' she said, then touched me lightly on the arm and motioned towards the door.

'It was a pleasure meeting you too, Larry,' I said as I retreated, knowing that I hadn't made much of an impact and wishing that I could erase the tape of this passage in time and begin over, having prepared beforehand something witty and interesting to say.

He just nodded.

'I'm sorry about that,' said Deirdre as she quietly closed the door behind us, 'but that's Lawrence, that's just the way he is. Don't be put off.'

'I wasn't put off.'

'We're up here,' she said, pointing up the stairwell and beginning to climb. 'Lawrence is actually really excited about you joining the company. He was very impressed with your application.'

'Really?'

'Oh yes,' she continued. 'Most people are with the company for months before they meet him. I think he came in this morning especially to meet you.'

'I feel privileged,' I said, regretting more intensely my failure to make an impression.

'You should,' she said. 'Anyway, we're here.' We stepped out onto the top floor of the building, which was split into three rows of cubicles, each row consisting of four compartments on either side of a dividing panel. Deirdre led me to a cubicle at the end of one of the rows. It had a view overlooking the street. A four-barred metal grille covered the window.

'And this,' she said, 'is your desk. It's not much, I know, and I'm sorry it's so cramped, but we're kind of stuck for space as it is. I did get you a window, though, which most people here would kill for.'

'Thanks,' I said, sitting down and swivelling in my chair. On the desk there was a monitor, a CPU tower, a phone, and a neat stack of folders. I looked out the window. I saw old warehouses, pubs, terraced homes, and, in the distance, the elevated hoardings of the Tara-to-Pearse-Street train line. The earlier scraps of cloud had gathered into long, thick packs that loped along in front of the sun; bands of shadow and light passed across the view.

'Now I'm really sorry to have to do this,' Deirdre said, 'but I have a meeting that I have to be at and it'll more than likely keep me all morning. But I've left you some reading to do'—she nodded at the files—'which should keep you going for a few hours. I'll be back at lunchtime and we'll go get something to eat and talk in detail about your role and then this afternoon there's this branding seminar that I'd really like you to attend with me.'

'Sounds good.'

'I hope it's not too overwhelming for your first day.'

'I'll get used to it.'

'You'll have to: it's like a madhouse around here sometimes. Right, I'm out of here.'

'Bye,' I said. She backed off, a little hesitantly. I watched her until she turned and disappeared around the end of the row, then followed with my ears the sound of her rummaging somewhere nearby; a few minutes later she called another goodbye to me and left.

Silence. I stood up and looked across the segregated room. No one else seemed to be in. I sat down, pulled myself towards the desk, selected the top folder, opened it, and began to read.

*

I had been back in the country only a couple of months, having returned in June from an eighteen-month sojourn in the States. After landing I gave myself a few days to recover from the jetlag, then spent the next week dispatching my CV to every Dublin-based recruitment agency and IT company listed in the *Golden Pages*, and the following three weeks attending an interview every second day: fecund times.

Before each interview I had donned my charcoal grey wool suit (which I reserved for interviews and funerals) with as much solemnity as if I were putting on an ecclesiastical vestment and preparing to enter the sanctum of some unpropitiated divinity. No, more accurate to say that each time I'd put on that suit I'd been putting on a costume—if I have learned anything during my career it is that a job interview is, essentially, a performance; to succeed, to negotiate its formalities, its nuanced disposition of player and theme, one has to be an actor. Or, at least, one has to act, to put on an act.

The trick is to gauge what kind of performance is required. Do you pitch it low-key or full-on? Do you project enthusiasm or nonchalance? Do you let the interviewer do the hard work, explaining why you should work for their company, or do you do all the talking, trying to impress as you enumerate your achievements, your interests, your academic record?

I seem, without quite knowing how, to have developed a knack for the job interview. Of the seven interviews I did that June I had three job offers as a return on the investment of my time.

I chose to join Aisling.

It was—let me see: one, two, three, four, five—my fifth job in four years.

*

My first job was with *Wake.com*, an 'online magazine of radical explorations in new culture'. Established by two young journalists who couldn't secure permanent positions with any of the big newspapers in Dublin, *Wake* had ambitions to become an Irish *Wired*.

I started with them on a part-time basis during the spring term of my final year at college, after responding to an ad that had been pinned to a noticeboard in my faculty. I thought I'd be doing writing or sub-editing, something journalistic like that, but those tasks were all being handled by the founders and a few of their equally freelance friends. What they did need, though, was someone to prepare their articles for uploading; I protested that I knew nothing about that sort of thing. *You'll learn*, they said—and I did (I picked it up mostly from a study of the source code of other websites). But more than coding, what I really learned was the philosophy of the site. The founders, Bill Gibbs and Robert Pound, believed in the revolutionary potential of the Web. They thought that it could prise open the 'global communications hegemony'. *Information is power*, they'd say, *and since we're taking back the means of distributing information* ... well, it followed that they were the vanguard of a revolution in individual and social consciousness that would replace the old dominator hierarchies with new webs of consensual egalitarian interaction.

I will admit that I was caught up in their fervour, so I was delighted when, after I finished my exams, the boys took me on full-time, paying my wages with seed capital from a business enterprise scheme. There were four permanent staff: myself, Bill and Robert, and Tricia, the office administrator, working out of a room in an incubation centre just off Baggot Street. It was tight, with three desks and two computers between the lot of us; but we hardly noticed, and, besides, we had luxuries: a cafetière and a knackered stereo that both belonged to Bill. We worked hard, bringing in tapes and CDs to provide a soundtrack, and fuelling ourselves with coffee bought at cost from an importer (and roaster) of gourmet beans who operated out of a unit on the floor below us.

But what I remember most about my time with *Wake* is not the work, nor even the people, but the way in which I would go walkabout on the Web whenever I got some time on one of the computers. I found myself drawn to the Net's stranger recesses, which were plentiful even then, the cranks determined to get their messages out before the crackdown came: stories of alien abductions and close encounters; spiritual experiences, visions, hallucinations; new religions; old religions spruced up; prophecies; earth mysteries and cryptozoology and crop circles; alternative histories of the world; theories of junk science, so called (cold fusion, anti-grav technology, zero-sum vacuum electricity); exposés of the military-industrial complex. I would sometimes read until one or two in the morning, the surfaces of my eyes desiccated by the glare of the computer screen, but my mind humming with the beautiful, twisted ludicrousness of it all. When I did eventually leave, I'd walk home through a city that seemed larger than it had before, wondering if the occasional person I passed had tales and opinions as odd and astounding as those I'd encountered online.

I pestered Bill and Robert to let me write a column for the magazine about all this stuff, and they eventually gave in, although it upset them to think that the Web could be used to communicate such frivolous information; not even information: *nonsense*.

I did not think it was nonsense; I thought it showed the myriad ways in which people could make sense of the world and I intended to argue as much in my column, which I had named 'The Pendulum'.

I wrote exactly one column before I left the magazine.

*

Deirdre asked me about *Wake* at our interview.

Her question made me realise how infrequently I now thought about my time there. It seemed like an unreal, even somewhat fantastical, interlude between finishing college and landing my first 'real' job. Same with Bill and Robert, and Tricia, too. When I heard a song or listened to an album from that summer I sometimes thought about them, and wondered what they were doing now, but only in an abstract way. I found it hard to bring them solidly to mind. They seemed more like people I had dreamt about—ghostly and intangible—than people I had actually worked with.

I have sometimes thought that *Wake* was in fact something

I'd made up, a fiction I had included in an early CV to bulk it out—or a fib I'd once told at an interview—that had mutated over the years into something I believed in almost as much as if it were true. But no, that can't be the case, because my brief time with *Wake* was often held against me, especially by interviewers. I wouldn't have concocted a story that tended to reflect badly on me.

Deirdre glanced down at my CV. 'You only worked there for a few months,' she said, making her statement function simultaneously as an enquiry and an accusation. I perfectly understood that, if interpreted in a certain way, the fact of my short tenure at Wake might make it look as if I had no staying power. This is not a trait you want to advertise to prospective employers. It was a weakness in my CV that I recognised. Deirdre's enquiry required a careful response. I had one prepared.

'The site was,' I said, with what I hoped was a note of regret, 'a bit before its time. We wanted to create a magazine that would do for Ireland what *Wired* did for the US, but we couldn't get anyone to sponsor the site or buy advertising space, so when the seed money ran out I had no choice but to move on.'

'That's a shame.'

'If it was now there'd be VCs queuing up to fling money at us.'

As if it had been only about the money. As if Bill and Robert had not thought that they were in it to tell new stories about the world, stories about a new world. They had no idea what they were doing, though, commercially. Their business model changed weekly in an effort to attract investment—from straightforward 'pull' magazine to push content provider to Virtual Community to online sub-cultural portal site. None of it convinced. At the tail end of that summer, I had sat in on a meeting during which Bill and Robert had tried to convince some money-men of the merits of pumping a little more capital into the project. The money-men listened and went away and came back saying that they were interested, but that they'd need to be further convinced of *Wake*'s long-term viability before they'd release any funds.

I understood then that the magazine didn't have a future. So when I saw a government department advertising in *The Irish Times* for an Internet administrator I applied and, when I was offered the position, resigned from *Wake* with regret but no small measure of alacrity.

'Tell me about your next job,' said Deirdre.

This answer too I had prepared. Like a folktale, the fundamentals remained the same each time it was told, but the details changed, stock phrases and incidents rearranged to accommodate the dispositions of the audience and the mood of the teller.

'I was hired by a government department,' I said, 'to advise on their Internet strategy. As a consultant. They'd set up a website about six months before I'd joined, but there was a feeling that the content was pretty inaccessible and not particularly representative of the department. So they decided to hire someone for a couple of months who not only had the necessary technical skills but who could also write, someone with a background in journalism who could set up the site so that it was easy to access and easy to update, while also effectively communicating the department's ethos.'

'Sounds fascinating,' said Deirdre flatly; I couldn't tell if she was being genuine or sarcastic.

'It was,' I replied in as equally flat a tone, bouncing the task of interpretation back to her. I wondered whether Deirdre truly believed what I'd just told her or whether she was merely impressed with the savviness of my response. She had surely done interviews in her time, used the same tricks I was using.

'And then you moved on again, I see. To one of the universities.'

'That's right.'

'To do what?'

'Pretty much the same thing,' I said blithely, 'but for more money.'

'More money?' She hooked my eyes with an amused and triumphant glance. She knew that I had said the wrong thing, and was curious to see how I might extricate myself. Check: to her, and game gets interesting. Even more interesting when she added, 'Had your contract expired?'

'Almost,' I said carefully, but not so carefully as to suggest that I knew I'd made a mistake. 'My contract had almost expired but that isn't what made me jump ship. You know how government departments work: there's a lot of bureaucracy and I was mostly just implementing someone else's directives. I didn't have a lot of input there, but with the university I got to plan and develop their whole web policy from scratch, almost.'

'I see,' she said, with less of an edge than previously. I had moved out of danger. It's a delicate game to play, the job interview. The dilemma is that the interviewer wants you to come work for her—if you fit her profile—and couldn't care less that this will involve you abandoning your current employer but, at the same time, she doesn't want you to seem too mercenary. Reveal to her your genuine reasons for leaving your present position (such as 'I'm bored there' or 'You're offering me more money' or 'My boss is just really painful to deal with') and your forthrightness will almost certainly guarantee that you won't be hired. The secret, I have found, is to praise your old job while at the same time drawing attention to its shortcomings. My favourite spin is to suggest that my current position is hindering my ambitions. Prospective employers don't like you to be greedy for money, but they don't mind at all if you seem greedy for hard work.

'I'd achieved all I felt I could achieve,' I added, to emphasise the point. 'It was time to move on.'

'To the job with the university?' she asked, checking her notes.

'Yes.'

'Where you only managed to last a year?' This was said without missing a beat or glancing at my CV. She had done her homework; she was trying to figure out something about me.

'There was an offer of a job in Boston that I couldn't turn down.'

'The job with Algonquin Inc.?'

' "Building a Global Community of Creative Individuals." '

'Sorry?'

'That was their by-line. The business plan was to build a virtual community of artists.'

'And how long did you work for them?'

'A year.'

'As their webmaster?'

'Mostly. I also did a bit of moderating on the message boards. It was a small company: everyone pitched in wherever they were needed.'

'And you left them because ...?' She left the question hanging. She was certainly making me work hard.

'I didn't really leave them,' I said, 'it was more like they left me: the company went bust.'

'I'm sorry to hear that.'

'Don't be,' I said, moving my hand dismissively. 'Just one of those things. It's not a big deal in the States. If a company goes down, you join another—or start your own—and keep going until you hit the jackpot.'

'What happened after Algonquin? You didn't return to Ireland immediately.'

'I temped for a while, then went travelling around the country for a few months.'

This information triggered what I sensed was her first unscripted reaction. She smiled at me with her eyes as well as her mouth.

'Really?' she asked, her edge almost entirely blunted.

'Really,' I said.

'Did you get to see the whole country?' she asked.

'As much as I could,' I said, responding to her enthusiasm with some enthusiasm of my own, but still careful not to give too much away: I didn't really reveal what I thought or felt about America, but I did run through my itinerary for her.

'That sounds like quite a trip,' she said when I'd finished.

'I'd always wanted to do it,' I said, 'and I had the money and the opportunity—'

'So why not?'

'Exactly.'

'Would you do it again?'

I'd been anticipating this question, knowing that she would, like other interviewers, want to establish whether I was infected with wanderlust and, if so, to what extent; whether I was liable to disappear in six months to go backpacking around south-east Asia or South America or wherever.

'Eventually,' I said, as if I hadn't really thought about it, as if it were at best a minor priority.

'But you'd like to go back to the States again?'

'Absolutely: I love the States.'

'We've just opened an office in Manhattan, you know.'

'Yeah, I read about that in the papers. What's it like?'

'I've never been.'

'To Manhattan or the new office?'

'Both. Neither.'

'You should go,' I said, then added the first wholly truthful and unparsed statement I had made to her: 'New York is an amazing city.'

'I'll go,' she said. 'I just need an excuse.' She laughed and I smiled. Turn the conversation around to them: number one rule of interviews. Number one rule of seductions, too.

*

My reading was interrupted by the appearance of a head above the partition separating my desk from the adjoining row of cubicles.

'Hey,' said the head, perching its chin on the panel. Male, with close-cut hair and a comically sly look on the face; and it was this expression—and the fact that I couldn't see anything of the body below the neck—that made me think that I was talking to something straight out of *Sesame Street* or *The Muppets*.

'Hey,' I replied, clenching my jaws in an effort not to smile or laugh.

'What's funny?' he asked.

'Nothing,' I said. 'I just didn't expect to see a head appear like that.'

He smiled, and his slyness suddenly seemed not at all comical: I realised that at least part of his motivation for popping up like that had been to give me a shock.

'My name is Tom,' he said.

'Eoin,' I replied, wary now.

'I know. Deirdre asked me to help you get settled in, but she probably didn't mention that, did she?'

'No.'

'Typical. She hopes that if she keeps pretending I don't exist that I'll just disappear one day—poof!—and stop hassling her.'

He moved as he talked. I tracked the progress of his head along the partition until it turned into my row and I saw that it was attached to a lean, broad-shouldered body—a rugby player in his teens, or ought to have been. I certainly thought I detected a Schools' accent, although not one he'd picked up at any of the colleges in Dublin; most likely he'd attended a college down the country: Garbally perhaps, or Roscrea.

'I used to do your job, you know,' he said, pulling over a chair from the empty cubicle next to mine and settling into it.

'Really?'

'Not for very long, though. I was moved onto different projects fairly quickly.'

'Promoted?'

'Promoted sideways. Communications isn't really my forte.'

'What is your forte?'

'I'm a programmer, Jim,' he said, 'not a writer.'

I tried to come up with a cognate pop culture reference with which to riposte, but couldn't think of anything. He didn't seem to notice: he began showing me where he'd stored the files relevant to my position on the LAN, the username and password I'd need to use to access the network (and my email and the Internet, too). When he'd finished he asked if I had any questions. I said no and then he asked what I thought of the company so far.

'I've only been here for an hour,' I protested.

'Give your first impressions, then.'

I wondered if this was a test, if Tom had been sent by Deirdre or Larry to conduct one final test of my suitability, or had perhaps taken it upon himself to perform this task: the company snitch, although he didn't seem the type.

'It seems very empty,' I said, choosing to give a safe answer. 'Where is everyone?'

'Probably at meetings,' he said, 'or they pulled a late one last night and are sleeping in.'

'You're allowed do that?'

'Oh sure,' said Tom casually. 'But that can't be your first impression. You must have some kind of feeling; everyone has some kind of gut feeling about a place.'

Gut feeling. I thought of my earlier nausea, suddenly realising that it had calmed itself without my noticing. I had had a similar nausea on the first morning of every job I'd ever taken, which had likewise passed. I said as much to Tom.

'You're very politic,' he said, sounding disappointed. 'I heard you met Larry this morning.'

'He's in the boardroom,' I said.

'*Was* in the boardroom,' said Tom, 'he's gone again now. So what happened?'

'We shook hands.'

'He didn't regale you with one of his parables, did he?'

All this time we had been sitting side by side, looking not at each other but at the computer screen. I turned now to assess his face. He turned to accept my scrutiny. He seemed serious enough.

'Parables?' I asked indifferently.

Tom turned his face back to the screen. I continued to look

at his profile. 'It's Larry's thing,' he said; 'one of his things. Ever since he found God he's become fond of greeting newbies with some kind of empowering, new-agey parable shite.'

'Didn't get one of those.'

'Don't feel left out: you will soon. It's inevitable in this place.'

'What do you mean by "found God"?' I asked after contemplating for several seconds how I should phrase the question.

Tom sighed. 'Larry was always a bit of a fucking hippie, you know, but then he went to some seminar which totally blew his mind and now he thinks he can change the fucking world.'

'What seminar?' I hadn't gotten any sense of this from my earlier chat with Larry.

'You'll find out soon enough: the story of Larry's conversion pretty much forms the centrepiece of the Aisling's induction course.'

'I hate induction courses,' I said, admitting myself a little honesty—though mostly to assess how Tom would react.

'Wait till you've done ours,' he said. 'I think hell is very probably an eternal induction course.'

I laughed, asking, 'Should you be telling me any of this?' I felt that Tom was someone I might eventually come to like, but was nonetheless suspicious of his motives.

'What should I be telling you?'

'Isn't it usual on a person's first day in a new job for everyone to tell you how great it is working for the company, how nice everyone is, how much fun you'll have: that kind of thing?'

Tom turned from the computer to take my gaze again. 'Listen, Eoin,' he said, 'Larry is always banging on about the power of honest communication. This is me communicating with you honestly.'

'I appreciate that,' I said, the only thing I could think of saying.

*

Deirdre and I talked about my role over lunch, but not in any great detail: just the basics, an outline. When we returned to the office after the branding seminar, however, she commandeered an empty meeting room and I listened as she explained exactly what it was she expected of me. By the time we were finished it was nearly seven o'clock but Deirdre didn't go home, so neither did I. Besides, I already had a long to-do list to get stuck into: type up a transcript of the seminar from Deirdre's dictaphone record; write a comprehensive description of my role, as I understood it; continue my reading, take notes, and prepare to begin work on what Deirdre had identified as my top priority: the 'Story of Aisling', a sort of Ur-document to which all Aisling staff members could refer when looking for officially sanctioned information to insert into their sales letters, or their project proposals, or whatever.

I didn't resent having to work late. I accepted that it was part of the game you played when you joined a new company. A friend once assured me that if you are seen to arrive at work early and leave late, you will make it difficult for people, particularly management, to categorise you as a poor worker, regardless of the overall inadequacy of your performance. A useful thesis, and one that I have through personal experience come to believe to be more or less true: the appearance of hard work is most of the time as pleasing to your superiors as actual hard work.

In the States, of course, this observation isn't so much a thesis as a principle of natural law. At Algonquin Inc., people rarely left before nine and even that was considered an early night. Every evening in the office we played the same game of Time Chicken, that old joke ('Taking a half-day, are we?')

directed at you if you were the first to crack and left at ten or eleven or twelve, exhausted, had had enough, knowing that it would take you an hour to get home and you'd have to be out of bed again by six to make it back into the office for eight the following morning.

I suspect that the majority of my colleagues at Algonquin were mostly idling at their workstations with no work to do other than the work of making an impression. I certainly was, my features and posture composed to make it appear as if I was working, when in fact I was web-surfing or catching up on personal email, work-related material prominently displayed on screen just in case a supervisor happened to glance over as they walked by.

I had perfected this technique during my tenure with the government department. There had certainly been no compelling professional reason for me to put in all the extra hours that I had: the work I'd been required to do I had completed during a regular working day. But there had also been little enough to entice me home, which at the time was a tatty bedsit in the basement of a Victorian redbrick in Ranelagh. It cost me thirty-five pounds a week, a sum I handed over to the landlord each Friday evening at seven-thirty when he presented himself in the entrance hall of the house so that each tenant could in turn offer him their rent and be ticked off in his little pocket book. He had made it clear when letting me the room that I would have to have a good reason to miss this weekly ritual, so to avoid unpleasantness I usually made myself available. But it was the only work night I would spend at home. Every other evening, I'd stay at my desk. Doing research. For a book.

My time with *Wake* had given me an ambition and, after I'd left, I had resolved to live hermit-like for a year or more—eighteen months, as long as it took—in order to achieve it: viz, to write a novel. I thought I had found my subject in the Web, you see, but, each weekend, when I would try to distil something from the printouts of a week's surfing, strewn before me on the table in the bedsit, I'd write nothing. Instead I'd stare out of the single window in the room, contemplating my tiny rectangle of sky. Or I'd write something, and then violently cross it out at once.

I seemed to have no idea how to write what I wanted to write about, even though I could picture it in my head, like the plan of an enormous building that I didn't have the *nous* to design properly or the patience to construct. My ambition was too large for me. It seemed futile: the world is too huge for the kind of containment I sought and anyway the things I came across on the Web made me realise that the book I wanted to write was being written, but not by one person—by multitudes. The Internet seemed to me to be like the ultimate cut-up novel, culture-sized, global and real; true and untreated and not the artifice of a single junked-out novelist. I loved the fact that on the Web everything was connected to everything else; I loved the weird collisions and linkages between information, how a word or phrase gnomically highlighted would lead you to some factoid you'd never have imagined. An ecology of minds, of words, in which each element depended for its existence on the existence of everything else in its environment.

I wondered where all these stories had come from, and whether they had been articulated before. The lunatic fringe, I thought, collapsing in upon the centre; or the return of the culturally repressed. I thought, too, of the anonymous and pseudonymous pamphlets that had circulated, post-Gutenberg, throughout Europe in the years just before and just after 1600, pamphlets purveying the same essential stories as the sites I loved exploring, and motivated by an identical chiliastic fervour, by the same idea of one world in the process of dying and passing away in preparation for the coming into being of a new and perfected existence. But whereas those Renaissance tracts had preached doom for all but a select elite, the modern prophets forecast an imminent transformation that would include everyone, everywhere, without exception.

I'm not saying that I believed these new prophets; I thought the stories they told were fictions. But what fictions! They seemed to me the very essence of fiction; my delight in them came not out of any thought of the truth they might embody, but in the realisation that they signalled that an entire world existed in parallel to the one I took for granted, inhabited by people who went to work every morning, loved, shagged, had children, divorced, visited their parents at Christmas, but people who, nonetheless, refused to accept that the world worked in exactly the way—or would develop in the direction—that most everybody else thought that it would.

Yet even as the writing stalled, my fascination with the Web grew; it might even have become an addiction, I don't know. I do know that I continued to stay late at work during the week—and went in most weekends, too. I stopped returning calls from my family and those few friends of mine who were still living in Ireland. And I interacted with no one except my colleagues and then only grudgingly and as necessity dictated. One Saturday, however, whilst shopping for groceries in Mortons, I bumped into a friend from college who had recently returned from a year in London. He was having a welcome-back party in the flat he'd just moved into, to which he invited me. I told him that yes of course I'd come along, having no intention at all of turning up, something I said to get rid of him, only to find myself, six hours later, standing at his door, carrying with me a bottle of wine and a resolution to break out of my rut.

Maybe I had had an inkling, because I met someone there: a woman.

'Friend of Miles?' she asked.

'From college,' I replied.

'Same course?'

'I'm afraid so. And you?'

'I've just graduated.'

'No, I mean how do you know Miles.'

'My sister is going out with his brother.'

'My name is Eoin,' I said.

'Erin,' she said. 'Where do I know you from?'

*

At ten that evening the quiet on the top floor of the office, where only Deirdre, Tom and I remained, was broken by the ringing of the phone on Deirdre's desk.

'Hi,' she answered, sounding weary. 'Yes, I know I said I'd be home early tonight ... yes, I know ... I'm waiting for a call from Lawrence ... fine, fine, I'll talk to you soon.'

She shut down her computer and stood up. 'I have to go home,' she declared. 'If Lawrence calls tell him he can reach me on my mobile. I'll have it switched on until eleven-thirty.'

'Of course,' said Tom, but after Deirdre had left he popped his head above the partition. 'You can go home now too,' he said. It sounded more like an order than a suggestion.

'I've just a little bit more reading to do.'

'Bollocks,' he said, 'you were only staying late to impress Deirdre and she's gone. The only person you're impressing now is me, and that's not going to do you much good—even if I was impressed, which I'm not.'

Tom's tone had more mockery than provocation in it, but I still had no idea how to react to his declaration. I had since that morning been speculating on Tom's agenda. He seemed to be testing me, probing in a systematic way; even now his look was hardly belligerent—it was more curious, disinterested, poised to measure how I might respond. I was caught cold in the abdomen by a fear: a gut reaction. A reaction to what? The possibility of entanglement in office politics, I suppose. However good I like to think I am at playing the game of interviews I have found that I am not nearly so adept at playing the game of office politics. I suspect that it has something to do with the fact that an interview is primarily a tactical engagement, rarely lasting longer than one or two rounds, whereas office politics demands a more long-term, strategic temperament. I don't seem to possess that disposition, nor have I ever had any inclination to develop it. I had not, up until then, stayed in any job long enough for it to matter.

Yet I was beginning to feel that Aisling could be different, that I could really like it here, stay as long as they'd have me. Based on what? A feeling, perhaps a gut feeling.

'What if Larry wants to get in touch with Deirdre?' I asked.

'Larry always seems to be able to get Deirdre,' he replied, winking. 'He's a resourceful man.'

'Oh,' I said. We stared at each other.

'Well,' said Tom, blinking first, 'I'm out of here. I'll show you how to set the alarm and lock the security door.'

'That's OK,' I said, 'you're right, I've finished everything I needed to do.'

As we descended the stairs to reception, Tom said, 'You never did tell me what your gut feeling was about the place.'

'I don't believe in gut reactions,' I said.

'How can you not believe in gut feelings?' he said to me over his shoulders. 'They're not fables like the tooth fairy or Marxist economics.'

'I mean that I don't believe they can be trusted.'

'Well, that's different. That's the start of something.'

'The start of what?'

'An interesting conversation, maybe.'

We had reached the reception area. 'Listen,' I said, 'I don't know what your agenda is, and I don't know why you want to know this, or who you're going to share it with, but my gut reaction is that Aisling, in its fundamentals, is no different from any other company I've ever worked for, and that any quirks it might possess have yet to reveal themselves.'

I was worried that he would suspect that I'd been rehearsing this speech, but all he said was, 'I don't have an agenda. But we do have our quirks. Let me show you something.'

He led me across reception to a door almost hidden behind Sheila's station.

'*Voilá* the Library,' he said, throwing open the door. Inside, a room that was little bigger than a walk-in wardrobe. Its three walls were lined from floor to ceiling with shelves packed tight with books.

'That's a lot of books,' I observed lamely.

'Whenever an Aisling consultant has some downtime between projects,' he said with an iambic rhythm that made me think *he'd* made this speech before or had also been rehearsing it all evening, 'he or she is encouraged to come in here and select a book they haven't read before to take away and study. Have a look.'

He switched on the light and then stepped back so that I could squeeze past him.

'There are books in there', said Tom from behind me, as I scanned the titles, 'about astrology, the Enneagram, meditation, yoga, Tai Chi, Qi Kong, creative visualisation, pranayana breathwork, focusing, shamanic vision quests, affirmations, chakras, crystal healing, holotropic consciousness, Platonic and neo-Platonic philosophy, modern continental philosophy, Buddhist philosophy, the Renaissance Art of Memory, morphological fields and every other kind of mumbo-fucking-jumbo there is.'

I had read, or read about, most of the books on display in the room, but I thought it better not to admit to that. I thought it better in fact to say nothing all, to keep my back turned.

'There's almost nothing in there about business,' he said plaintively, after a beat, and for the first time since meeting him, I felt like I had gained an edge on Tom. If we were engaged in a contest, I thought, then I might as well try to score some fucking points off him, even the match up a bit.

'Speaking of questions that were never answered,' I said, turning back around, 'you haven't said yet why you're telling me all this.'

'I have a feeling about you,' he said flatly.

'A gut feeling?'

'Yeah a gut feeling, a gut feeling that you might actually buy into all of this bullshit.'

I crossed my arms and raised my eyebrows: *So?*

'Fine,' he said, 'all I'm saying is that it's just a job. Don't let yourself be brainwashed, because it's not your life, and it's absolutely not your soul.'

*

A few minutes later I waited with Tom outside the office as he locked down the steel security barrier over the front door. He'd asked me to wait around while he did this because once or twice some skangers from the Chateau at the end of the street had shadowed him during the operation and he hadn't felt comfortable.

Chateau? I was confused until Tom pointed it out to me: how the line of high buildings on either side of us guided one's eyes away from the river and towards the long, squat residential block that capped the street: aka the 'Chateau'. The face of this building was entirely functional—unadorned with any rococo flourishes—but in the haze of the streetlights it too reminded me of the exterior of the sort of large French manor house you might approach via a formal driveway.

'I appreciate this,' he said as he snapped the padlocks shut.

'No problem.'

'Listen, don't ever take what comes out of my mouth too seriously. I usually don't mean half of it.'

He stood up, done.

'Which way are you heading?' I asked.

He jabbed his thumb towards the south. 'I'll cut up to Pearse and get a DART from there.'

'What about the skangers?'

'I'll be fine once I'm moving. And you, which way are you heading?'

I nodded towards the river.

'Well, see you tomorrow,' he said.

'Seeya.'

He moved off with large, bobbling strides that had him

almost jogging. I checked my watch and realised, after a little calculation in my head, that I'd missed the last train home by a good half-hour. The next bus didn't leave Eden Quay for another forty-five minutes. Not wanting to stay standing where I was for fear of the skangers, and having no key to get back into the office, I went searching for some place still serving coffee.

Case Study II

(Source: Aisling internal emails)

To: lawrence.cooley@aislingltd.com
From: eoin.cullen@aislingltd.com
Subject: Transcript of Dr Chuck Sweeney's branding
seminar, Part I
Date: 06/08/1999

Larry,

Find attached a transcript of the first half of Dr Sweeney's
speech. The second half will follow tomorrow.

Call me if you have any questions.

Eoin

Brands and the Meaning Dimension

Transcript of a lecture delivered by Dr Chuck Sweeney
(Director of the Barton Institute for Branding Studies)

What is a brand? We are surrounded by so many brands that the answer to this question seems self-evident: we just *know* what brands are, intuitively, without having to think about them.

And yet, you know, there is a sense in which it is very easy to define a brand. A brand is meaning. It is, if you'll excuse the academic turn-of-phrase, a 'concrete sign'.

Now we are not academics. (*laughter*) We don't really want to understand brands. What we really want to do is ensure that our brands achieve maximum dominance of the available market space. (*more laughter*)

Which is why I'm not only going to help you understand brands this afternoon, I'm also going to show you how to turn this knowledge to your advantage.

So, brands are meaning. More than that, they are meaning with a purpose. They tell a story. In fact, good branding is about creating a powerful, meaningful, resonant narrative around your company, a narrative in which you will embed the story of each individual product or service you sell.

Why is this important? Because we are moving into a post-consumer economy. People—by which I mean consumers—are no longer content to be defined simply or solely by the act of shopping or by the monetary value of the objects they purchase. These concerns are still important, but they are superseded by a larger concern, which is articulated by consumers in the question, 'What part am I playing in the story of this product or service?' Your customers want to be involved in the unfolding story being told by your company; they want to be characters in the drama your brands are enacting; they want to be conduits for the values that your brands are embodying.

In other words, modern consumers no longer simply consume goods and services, they consume symbolic meanings.

Without dwelling too much on the sociological and economic reasons for this, I think we can safely say that it is a result of the fact that the West has pretty much solved the problem of providing the majority of its citizens with a decent standard of living. In America, for instance, most people haven't had to worry about the first two or three levels on Maslow's pyramid of needs since at least the 1950s.

And this development has had very interesting consequences. A mass of previously unused energy was directed at examining the old grand narratives by which we had lived. Not surprisingly, all those narratives—Christianity, communism, socialism, even pure, old-school capitalism; the original brands, if you will— shrivelled up under the glare of all that intense inspection.

What remained was a world of affluence *that had no meaning.*

But people need stories, as surely as they need nourishment, shelter and sex. Indeed, once those three basic needs are met, people will turn their attention to stories with the same energy and drive they previously gave to their quest for survival. And, of course, it is still a matter of survival, but the survival of intangible, psychological qualities such as self-knowledge and self-esteem.

Now the world, the Western world, has been deprived of great stories for the last twenty years or so—certainly for the last ten, since the fall of the Berlin Wall—which is where branding comes in. Successful branding sells great stories, sells a sense of identity, of belonging to something larger than oneself, of being involved with something meaningful beyond the Self. Good branding is about making people feel better about themselves: it's about selling salvation.

Or, as Scott Edby, the marketing director of Starbuck's, has so eloquently put it, the successful branding strategy aims to align a company 'with one of the greatest movements towards finding a connection with [a customer's] soul'.

And now we return to the question I posed at the beginning of my talk: What values should we communicate through our brands? The answer to this question is, I'm glad to say, very simple. The values that you should communicate are the same eternal values that resonate with people across generation and culture. The values that human beings have always striven to realise: freedom; beauty; gratification, sexual and otherwise; connection; individuality; creativity.

But good brands are not just about values—they are also about techniques for selling those values. After what you've heard so far, you probably won't be surprised when I inform you that these techniques are a mixture of ancient and modern psychology and are concerned primarily with bypassing the subject's ego and directly accessing their unconscious aspirations, what I call their 'value factory'.

But before I go into that, were there any questions about what you've just heard?

(*silence*)

[End of Part One]

To: eoin.cullen@aislingltd.com
From: lawrence.cooley@aislingltd.com
Subject: RE: Transcript of Dr Chuck Sweeney's branding seminar,
Part I
Date: 07/08/1999

eoin
that's great, but could you bullet point it for me, and the second
half too?
thanks,
larry

3. Vision:
The Aisling Philosophy of Business

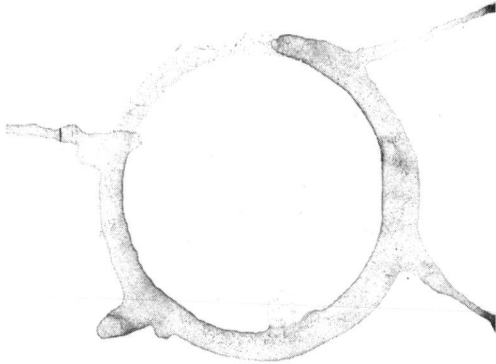

Even though Deirdre insisted that I would have to interview Larry before I could finish writing the story of Aisling, it was several weeks before I saw or even talked to him again. He assured me by email that he did want to meet; it was just that it was difficult for him to set aside the necessary time. A few days after the induction course, however, he sent a message to inform me that if I accompanied him as he flew from Dublin to New York the following Tuesday morning we'd be able to talk without interruption.

*

I thought the timing was suspicious but I was determined to nevertheless conduct myself like a professional. That is, I armed myself with information. But since the only official sources I had access to were press clippings, and the occasional hagiographical remark from Deirdre, it was to Tom I turned for full disclosure of the facts of Larry's life.

Given his behaviour on my first day in the company, I thought that the best I could have expected of Tom was a degree of civility. But our association was more than merely civil and although we rarely agreed on anything, we enjoyed each other's company; or, rather, I enjoyed his and he seemed to tolerate mine. Most days we were alone on the top floor of the office, and whereas we could have contented ourselves with silence, we actually spent much of our time arguing things back and forth across the paltry partition that separated our desks. If other people happened to be present we switched to email or Internet Messenger to continue our discussions. Sometimes we continued them outside the office, over a pint or two in O'Neill's. It was in O'Neill's, in fact, that Tom told me the story of Aisling's big break.

'The thing to remember about Larry,' he said, by way of a preface to his tale, 'is that before he became Jerry-fucking-Maguire he was a great salesman—I mean a really great salesman—and a really fucking first-rate grafter too. I bet no one has told you how he landed Aisling's first big contract, have they?'

I shook my head.

'Okay, he's just set up the company, right, and it's not going so well; he doesn't have any big names on the books, just piddling little SMEs who never pay on time, so there's fuck all money coming in. Then Larry hears—don't ask me how—that the chairman of one of Ireland's leading multinationals is vaguely interested in this Internet thing he's been hearing about, but doesn't really know what it could do for his business, if in fact it could do anything at all. Larry also hears that the multinational has sent out tenders to all the big consultancies, but hasn't been much impressed by their responses.

'Now Larry knows that he can do better. But there's a catch. The chairman exists in a completely different stratosphere to Larry. There's no way that the MD of a small consultancy will ever be able to bag a meeting with this man. So Larry does some digging and discovers that although the man is a complete maniac for work, he almost never misses his son's games of 5-a-side soccer, no matter what he's doing, or how busy he is.

'But there's another catch: Larry doesn't have any children; he doesn't know any children—he doesn't even have any nieces or nephews, *nada*; but he makes a few calls, and signs himself up as a member of the same soccer club as the chairman, which just happens to be looking for a coach for one of its underage teams. Not the same team the chairman's son is on, but still— close enough. Anyway, Larry presses the flesh and gets himself appointed as the new coach, which can't have been easy for a separated man with no sprogs of his own, but somehow he manages, no pun intended. The months go by. Larry and the chairman start to recognise each other; they say hello; they get to talking between shouting on their respective charges; and eventually the chairman, who finds Larry to be a sympathetic listener, tells him about his dilemma to which Larry modestly replies that he might have the solution, won't cost a fortune either, and right there on a muddy soccer pitch in South County Dublin the chairman hires Aisling as his company's Internet consultants, practically throws a blank cheque at Larry, he's so impressed by what he perceives to be Larry's integrity, and the rest is history: Aisling's big break.'

Tom paused after concluding his story, and then emphatically added, before I could say anything, 'Put that in your profile of Larry.'

'I will,' I said.

'Make sure that you bloody do,' he said, 'because that's the way it's done. It's about graft and luck and having the balls to go out there and nail down your deals.'

Not without some trepidation, I put this proposition to Larry soon after we had taken off. It was in effect my first question. I had my dictaphone turned on.

'It's not about graft,' said Larry. 'Or even luck. It's about trust, and self-belief.'

He glanced at me to make sure that I understood this distinction; I held his gaze and smiled, to let him know that yes, I was following.

'Let me give you a concrete example,' he went on, looking away (for which I was glad; my eyes had begun to moisten with the effort of maintaining a steady reciprocating stare) and adopting a tone of voice very different to the one I had heard him first employ; it was just as boisterous and full-bodied, but more moderate in expression—the sound of a wise man passing on his knowledge to a pupil, as opposed to someone riling a friend.

'Take branding,' he said, 'and this is something that your friend Doctor Sweeney never mentions, but the thing about branding is that the average consumer asks themselves just two questions when faced with a choice between competing brands: which is better value for money, and which do I trust more?

'Pricing is the easiest part of the equation to sort out: you make sure your price is roughly in line with your competitors; maybe a little less, maybe a little more, depending on your costs. Nothing too difficult there. Trust, on the other hand, is complicated. It's hard to get right, and it's hard to measure, but I think—and it's just my opinion, but I think I'm right about this—that if you charge more than your competitors but still manage to make the sale then you've established trust. The customer is telling you that he is willing to pay a premium for that trust. In fact, he's not really paying you for the product or service at all. He's actually paying you to ensure that once he's bought your commodity he never has to worry about the product breaking down or the service not delivering. He's paying you a premium for the privilege of not having to worry.

'And this is what Aisling is about. It's what we have to be about. We can't afford to charge less than the big consultancies. We simply wouldn't survive if we got dragged into a price war. We'd be annihilated. The one advantage we have over them is trust. But it's a big advantage. Do you know why? Because no one trusts the big guys. I used to work for one of them. I saw how the clients regarded us. We were a necessary evil, but no more than that. They needed our services, but they detested us and would have done without us if they could, but they couldn't: they were bound to us and by God we exploited that bondage. It was, frankly, an unequal and sadistic relationship and I began to question if it could be different, if there could be a more honest way of doing business, a more humane way of treating our clients, treating them as partners, for instance, not clients. I began circulating these proposals about injecting more transparency into our business relationships, but all I got in return were polite pats on the head—no one took me seriously—and I began to realise that the problem was institutional, not operational. The company was never going to change because it *couldn't* change; it would take just too much effort to overhaul decades of doing things the way they'd always been done. The obvious solution was to set up a small company offering essentially the same services, but doing everything better, quicker, and with more honesty. And that's exactly what I did. Aisling is exactly the sort of company I'd want to work for, doing exactly the sort of work I was doing with my former company, but doing it with some principles, with an eye to some goal other than simply making money.'

'What are our principles, Larry?' I asked. My voice sounded somewhat formless to my own ears. Uncertain. I badly wanted to project some potency, to make more of an impression than I had at our first meeting, but he was intimidating me—and not because he displayed any belligerent qualities, but precisely because he was being, on the contrary, so open, so confident, and so assured; he seemed alive, a fully formed spirit compared with what I felt was my own faltering work-in-progress.

'Openness,' he said without pausing: 'openness is our first principle. We don't lie and we don't make false promises. The second principle is respect: respect for ourselves, respect for the client, and respect for the context in which we operate.'

He counted off the points as he spoke, tapping a finger onto the arm of his chair for each one. 'Our third principle is flexibility. We change to meet the needs of the client, rather than forcing them to adapt to ours. They're the ones paying the money; it's only right that we adapt to them.

'Our fourth and final principle is vision. By this I simply mean that we know where we've come from, where we're going, and what we stand for.'

I expected that Larry would elaborate on what he meant by

this, as it seemed a rather clipped explanation for him, but he did not. I felt that he was waiting for me to respond.

'What *do* we stand for?' I asked, trying as far as I could to strain the nervousness out of my voice, to keep it sounding neutral, fair-minded, efficient: that's the impression I wanted Larry to take away with him.

'A whole new way of doing business, a way that will change the world.'

He again failed to voluntarily enlarge on his statement.

'That's ambitious,' I heard myself say.

'There's nothing wrong with being ambitious,' he countered.

'Were you always ambitious for Aisling?' I asked.

'Always,' said Larry. 'I knew exactly where I wanted her to go from day one.'

'Tell me more about those early days.' It was all I could think to say. The conversation had become stilted and it almost seemed as if Larry was deliberately interrupting the flow, in order to make me work for my information, in order to test me—but this was obviously just paranoia because, after taking a few moments, Larry started into another speech:

'At first Aisling was just myself, Padraig Finn, who's still with us, and Maeve Muckian, who is not. We had each managed to bring to Aisling one client from the companies where we'd worked, thinking that we could handle that, but it was just the three of us working on projects that had previously been the preserve of huge, well-resourced teams. We didn't even have an office for the first couple of months, so we based ourselves in my dining room—which is one reason for my separation, though that doesn't go in my profile; that's off the record.'

'Of course,' I murmured.

'Sometimes,' he continued, 'I wonder how we managed at

all. Looking back, it seems ludicrous that we should have tried to do everything ourselves. But we did. Apart from the programming, which we hired contractors to do, the three of us ran around managing everything else—budgets, implementation, scheduling, client management—*everything*. It was bloody hard work, but it was also a great learning experience. I suddenly found that I had to become competent in aspects of business that I'd only known previously in theory.'

'It sounds like it was a struggle.'

'It sure felt like a struggle at the time, trying to keep everything running smoothly and everyone happy, but looking back it was the perfect foundation. We grew as fast as we needed to grow.'

He said nothing further, looking instead at me in expectation of a response. 'Tell me more about Aisling's lucky break,' I said without thinking—just to say something, anything—and regretted my choice of words almost immediately as Larry replied with a quick, fierce and defensive retort:

'I've already said it had nothing to do with luck. It was the result of hard work and knowing exactly what we wanted. I had visualised Aisling working for a multinational, had seen clearly in my head how it could be achieved, had broken the process down into discrete steps, and had made sure that each of those steps was achieved. It was no surprise to me when we got that contract. I was delighted, of course, but not surprised. Surprise is for the unprepared.'

'Sounds very scientific,' I said, wincing inside at my banality, but thinking that's what he would want to hear.

'In a way,' he replied slowly, as if he was used to being misunderstood on this point, 'but it's an art, too. It's about approaching the world in a focused way, and achieving your goals systemically, rather than waiting for Fate to deliver what you want, which it might never do.'

I suppose this was Larry's creed, condensed. My reaction on hearing it stated so baldly was one of embarrassment; embarrassment for Larry, that he should believe such things, and embarrassment for myself, too, because I believed these things as well, or wanted to. Badly wanted to: before our flight together I may have known of Larry's beliefs mostly through Tom's homilies on the subject, but I had always defended what Tom clearly wanted me to excoriate and more than once he had accused me of being a willing dupe of Larry and his high priests.

'The "high priests"?' I had asked the first time he used the phrase.

Tom smiled in response with mock-despair, an expression he employed whenever he wanted to communicate to me just how much I had yet to learn.

'You do know, don't you, that Larry has outsourced the HR operations of the company?'

'I had no idea.'

'You haven't had any dealings with them ... yet.' Tom delivered the theatrical delay in the sentence with relish.

'HR are always bastards,' I said, to keep on his good side.

'But these are evil, New Age HR bastards,' he said, unplacated: 'they'll shaft you but still expect you to love them for it. How can you trust anyone who labels themselves a change-enablement specialist?'

'Is that what they call themselves?'

'No, that's what they claim they do. What they call themselves is Essentia Inc., the pretentious fucking twats, and they, my little Padawan, are Larry's high priests: the enforcers of his dogma.'

Back on the plane, Larry was once again waiting for me to

say something. 'How did you get interested in this whole area?' I asked.

'What whole area?'

'Self-development, that kind of thing.'

'I've always been interested in the Human Development Movement,' he replied with complete sincerity. 'The problem I've always had, though, and I'll be candid about this, is that I have struggled with applying the lessons I learned in that field to my business life.'

'And that's where Essentia come in?'

'That's exactly where Essentia come in.'

'How long have you been working with them?'

'Let me see. I've personally been working with them since I attended one of their seminars in 1996, but they've only been attached to Aisling for the past year. This is all covered in the induction course, you know.'

'I know,' I said, 'but I wanted to hear it from you.'

'You did the induction course recently, didn't you?'

'Just over a week ago,' I said, as calmly as I could, although it was the question I had been dreading since meeting him at the airport; the fact that he had asked it so informally only deepened my anxiety.

'What did you think of it?'

'I'm meant to be interviewing you,' I reminded him.

'I've talked enough for now. Turn off that tape recorder and tell me what you thought of our induction course.'

His enquiry sounded polite; he had asked inoffensively enough, and his tone suggested innocence, but I was sure news of what had happened had gotten back to him.

I had my version of events prepped, though.

I stopped recording.

*

Two Fridays prior to my flight with Larry, I and eleven others had been collected outside the Dublin office at 7 a.m. by a minibus that had then driven us out of the city along the N4. As we'd headed west, the dawn had decayed into a grey, over-cast morning and, past the turnoff for Maynooth (the city-bound traffic thinning out, the road ahead clearing out too), a mist had slithered like liquid porcelain in the fields, held back from the tarmac by the wire fences and crash barriers lining the motorway.

It was, all in all, a dispiriting morning on which to be head-ing to Kilcoyle House, Aisling's new retreat centre in County Sligo, for an induction course.

Purchased last year, read the information sheet that had been emailed to each inductee, *and nearing the end of an exten-sive programme of renovation, Kilcoyle House is the perfect location for a weekend that will introduce you to the company ethos and equip you with all the skills and knowledges you'll need to thrive in our fast-paced, initiative-based environment.*

I'd written this, mostly. Deirdre had emailed me a rough draft of the sort of thing she wanted, asking me to tidy it up for her. I retained certain of her phrases ('fast-paced', 'initiative-based', the clumsy poetics of the compound adjective) but most everything else I amended: structure, emphasis, pacing. I took particular care to change all her passive constructions into active clauses, which is the first thing I'd learned about business writing: never write in the passive—the active presupposes a more dynamic view of the world, and is therefore thought more likely to excite the reader.

Excite the reader. The second thing I learned about writing for business is that one should always write for a particular audience, but more than that: to write for a specific member of that audience, whom you should imagine as an idealised individual. For instance, when writing a mission statement for a blue-chip share issue prospectus you ought to suppose that you are addressing the ideal, Platonic version of the institutional investor: economically conservative, cautious, judicious. When composing a job advert, on the other hand, you would pitch your words to catch the attention of your ideal candidate, bringing to mind as you write an image of exactly the sort of person you would like to hire: poised, confident, presentable, with that hint of energy in his eyes—that direct, forthright stare suggestive of will, forcefulness and ambition.

I had largely developed this theory on my own through trial and error. I had been with Aisling only two weeks, however, when Larry emailed me a link to an article by an Essentia associate describing a revolutionary approach to business writing that the writer called the 'persona-based methodology'.

The writer of this article, citing as his precedents the amulets of the Hermeticists of Renaissance Florence and the sigils of Austin Spare ('the William Blake of the modernist movement in Britain'), likened this approach to an act of thaumaturgy: you fiercely visualise your desire, then cast it in the form of a spell in order to attract it to yourself. I spotted the flaw in this formula almost at once but, to be fair, the author was wise to it too: if one chooses the wrong persona to appeal to, or employs words, images, appeals, suggestions, facts, figures and/or calls-to-action that do not resonate with their values or self-image, then your charm will fail, the spirits will not heed your request, nothing will result.

The key to writing for a specific persona-type, then, is

research. One: you identify your target persona, understanding fully why you have chosen him or her to communicate with. There is really no point conjuring up a persona if there is no profit for you in attracting them in the first place.

Two: their likes, their dislikes. Read what they might read; value what they might value; acquire their language. It is a truism of this methodology that every 'type' has his or her own language, or, if that's too strong for you, uses language in his or her own way. A stockbroker is likely to use language in a way that differs from the way a programmer or a chemist or a marketing executive uses language, at least professionally.

Three: their values, for which read their aspirations. It is not one's duty to be normative. If a persona-type is acquisitive then write to that. The business writer must absent himself from the text. There should be no personality in the words, except that of the imagined persona.

This, again, was something that I had already learned myself. Dorothea, my manager at Algonquin, a former journalist and sub-editor, had emailed back all my early pieces for her with the same comment, or variations thereof, attached: 'too personal', she would write, or 'excise yourself here' or 'too much of *You*'. By the time I'd been let go, I had attuned myself so astutely to her requirements that I could write without her needing to edit my pieces beyond some basic proofing and copy-editing.

Dee was not nearly as demanding, mainly because she had not had Dorothea's formal training. Yet she had her own preferences, prejudices even, and, after a couple of months of writing for her, I was beginning to become accustomed to her requirements, and to mould my writing to her satisfaction. Actually, I ought to say to her and Larry's satisfaction, because

I knew that every item of written information about Aisling that was released publicly, and much that was circulated internally, had to be approved by him.

This, incidentally, is a piece of advice that the Essentia article failed to discuss: always write to your manager's prejudice. It's just common sense. To do otherwise is to invite constant revisions and endless back-and-forth and back-and-forth and back-and-forth edits until all sense in the piece has been diluted, rendered anaemic. Far better to gauge your manager's preferred style and adjust your writing accordingly. Dee's inclination was for a sort of breathless, run-together prose and I initially struggled with the task of putting together the adjective-dense pieces that she required; I still occasionally stumbled. I had not been entirely satisfied with the flyer I had written for the induction course, and neither had she. 'It'll do, though,' she'd said kindly. 'Not bad for something put together in a few hours.'

What persona had I had in mind when I'd written the email? I glanced around at the other people on the bus, none of whom I had met before, and wondered whether they had recognised themselves—the passionate, dedicated and creative co-architects of Larry's vision—as they had read the text.

If they had read it. They had most likely not, or, if they had, they'd scrolled through it once and retained little enough of its sense.

I didn't care. It didn't matter to me. That's the most important thing I've learned about writing for business: forget about it. It's transient. None of it lasts. It is done, dispatched, and then dies. Just dies away.

*

The road ran smooth and widely verged, bypassing or passing through the towns along the route—Mullingar, Edgeworthstown and Longford—and bringing us by boarded-up dancehalls, pet-food factories, abandoned cottages, and empty paddocks in which old oaks stood stately but alone, defrocked of their summer foliage. Occasionally we drove through banks cut out of hills too large or stubborn to go around, on the other side of which were long high vistas of the Midlands: drumlins and copses and rutted pastures, and glimpses of the Shannon with its myriad tributary lakes.

We also passed the occasional Big House, set back from the road behind high walls and thickets of tall, old trees. I wondered if Kilcoyle looked at all like any of those half-glimpsed structures. I had not seen any photographs of it, and when I had asked Dee how I ought to describe it for the flyer, she'd told me that it didn't matter, that the location in itself wasn't that important. Tom, on the contrary, had been eager to supply details.

'It's some big old Anglo-Irish mansion,' he said. 'Larry bought it on a whim. Basking, of course, wanted to turn the grounds into a golf course and the house into a hotel, but Larry thought it would make a great location for a corporate retreat centre.'

'Is it?'

'I wouldn't know—I've never seen the place. I hear, though, that the renovations are taking longer—and costing more—than anyone expected. Larry apparently wanted any trace of the original interior just torn out, all of it, thrown into a skip.'

'Can he do that?'

'He already has.'

'What about conservation? Surely you can't just do that.'

'Don't be so bloody naïve, Cullen,' he said bluntly: 'When you know the right people and have the right amount of money, you can do whatever the hell you like with your property: it's your constitutional right.'

'Well ...' I said, trying to think of something to say that would ameliorate my sense of having had another point scored on me by Tom, 'well, talk about ridding himself of the symbols of our oppression.'

'Don't mock: Larry's very sensitive about shit like that, growing up near the Border and all.'

'Christ,' I said, 'don't tell me that Larry's a Shinner.'

'Not that I know. I think he probably votes Labour, the fucking pinko, but he's still fond of reminding people that anything we have in this country was wrested from the grip of 700 years of occupation. Though I sometimes think he means the bishops as much as the Brits.' He took a sip of his coffee, then continued, 'But anyway you wouldn't recognise the place now. It's been stripped bare in preparation for being remade in the modern style.'

'I thought you said you hadn't seen it.'

'I haven't, but I've overheard Larry talking to the interior designers, and I've seen some of the plans.'

'Has anyone been down there yet?'

'You'll be the first,' he said with a laugh. 'The guinea-pigs.'

'Great.'

'It'll be more than great. Think about it: every induction course up till now has been held in some posh city-centre hotel, with lunch and dinner and a free bar afterwards. You, on the other hand, will have the pleasure of being driven halfway across the country to an old, run-down, half-renovated Big House, where you're liable to be fed gruel and stale bread in pursuit of some much needed character-building. You'll have a fantastic time.'

*

Although Kilcoyle House is located just outside Sligo town, it took a while for our driver to find it. He dead-ended us in a few cul-de-sacs before taking a left onto a road that he claimed just had to be the right one, though it didn't look the part, lined as it was by bungalows and two-storey townhouses. After half a mile, though, the houses gave way to an avenue of shrubs and stubby trees—hazel and birch and ferocious clusters of rhododendron— and then someone spotted a structure off to the side of the road and the driver said 'That's it' and someone else said 'Thank Christ' and we were turning in at an open stone gateway, not much larger than the gates of a modest farm, and proceeding down a short drive with more trees (larger now, beech and larch) to our left and a large paddock to our right, before parking up in front of a stolid, three-storey Georgian mansion.

I had expected to be more impressed. Perhaps it was the day, and the strangely uniform sky we had brought with us from the city: the sun coldly smouldering behind a film of cloud like a low-wattage bulb seen through a sheet of paper, infusing the landscape with the bored, shiftless light that is peculiar to Irish winters. But really the environs were lacking in a certain grandiosity, and the house itself was similarly undistinguished. It was not, moreover, in pristine condition. I noticed that its walls were pocked with scabs of lichen, that weeds were sprouting out from it in places, and that there was also what looked like a bullet-hole above the front door, its cracks radiating outwards and fracturing the faded family crest that capped the lintel.

This doorway was set maybe a metre off the ground at the top of a short flight of stairs. It opened as we were climbing out of the minibus. A man dressed in a sweatshirt and jeans emerged. He skipped down the steps towards us.

'Hello,' he said, when he'd reached our level, 'my name is Aengus. I'll be your facilitator for the weekend. Welcome to Kilcoyle House.'

We mumbled our hellos in return. He then asked us if we were hungry. The consensus was that we were.

'Excellent,' he said. 'I'll show you to your rooms, then let the kitchen know you're here. By the time you've settled in, brunch will be ready and waiting.'

He led us into the house and up a wide staircase to the second and third floors. The refurbishment of the house was more advanced than Tom's intelligence had suggested, but he had been right about the choice of styles. Nothing, as far as I could see, of the original character of the interior had been retained. The old floors and wainscoting, the rococo ceiling mountings and the bas-reliefs in the pediments above the doors had all been removed. In their place, light wooden floors; chunky furniture of maple, pine or white oak, accessorised with cushions and throws in primary colours; lots of light and space, abstract or minimalist paintings on the magnolia walls: we might have been in any building designed according to the rules of Shaker–Scandinavian fusion, and the bedroom to which I was shown might have been any hotel room in the world. There were no clues as to its location, except for the le Brocquy print above my bed and the view from the window, which looked southwards to a range of long, blue, ragged hills.

*

After brunch, during which he informed us that he was a consultant with Essentia, and head of the team responsible for managing Aisling's HR requirements, Aengus ushered us into a meeting room for an orientation talk, which was followed by a suite of personality tests that lasted for the rest of the afternoon.

In the evening, following supper, we hired some taxis to bring us into town, ending up towards the end of the night in some pub down on the riverbank. Here I found myself sitting beside a man in his late forties who had earlier introduced himself as Fintan O'Connor. I didn't say anything to him beyond hello (at this stage I was tired of chit-chat), but I sensed he wanted to talk to me. During my trip around the States I had often found myself sharing rooms or dormitories in dilapidated hostels and working joe's hotels with one or more unfamiliar men and I had developed the skill of being able to determine within a few minutes of making a man's acquaintance whether he was a talker or a listener or whether he just wanted to be left alone.

Given that I am by nature more of a listener than a talker, I was surprised at the high proportion of men who turned out to be the latter. I thought at first that it was a quirk of the American personality or a factor of the circumstances, the loquaciousness of men down on their luck, but I eventually became kind of paranoid about it, felt it might have something to do with me: some people just seemed compelled to tell me their stories.

I glanced up and his eyes were upon me. He smiled. 'What didya think of all that personality test stuff?' he asked.

'There was more to it than I'm used to,' I said, 'but it's not the first one I've had to do.'

'It's the first one I've ever done,' he said with a laugh, but it was an uneasy laugh. 'I felt like I was back doing me exams.'

'I don't think you can fail a personality test,' I said reassuringly, though I couldn't help adding, 'unless you're a sociopath or something, but even then I don't think they're set up to detect that kind of thing.'

'Hm.' I knew that I had said something that he hadn't cared to hear. We both swerved our gazes away from the other. 'It's just,' he said after a moment, 'that I felt I was giving away things about myself that I wouldn't like to share.'

'I understand how you feel,' I said, trying to re-establish some rapport.

'It's common, then,' he asked, 'this sort of thing, in these Internet companies?'

I shrugged my shoulders, to say *I guess so.*

'I've never worked in this kind of company before,' he said, then paused. I didn't say anything. He hadn't asked a question that demanded an answer, and the pause felt more like a space in which he could gather his thoughts than a gap into which I could direct an opinion.

'I joined the company I was with straight out of school after the Leaving Cert,' he continued, 'me father worked there too, you see. It's just what you done in those days when you'd grown up where I'd grown up, if you were lucky; it was that or take the boat. You went in on the shop floor, as it were, done a degree in the evening, if you had the inclination, all paid for by the company, but mostly you just put in your hours and collected your wages at the end of every month. You bought a nice house for your family, you went on a holiday every summer, you saw that your chisellers never went without, and you put a few squids aside for when you retired. You worked to give yourself things, but you didn't have to work too hard, do you see what I'm saying?'

'I see,' I said.

'I don't think you do,' he said. 'These high-tech firms are so different, all about making your millions and retiring before you're fifty. I'm nearly fifty myself. I'm not even sure why I left the company, but everyone was leaving, anyone with any kind of sauce in their heads was leaving, and telling me that I had to leave and get in while the going was still good and anyway I was head-hunted, so I couldn't really say no, could I?'

'What did you do at your old firm?'

'Production engineer, eventually: making chocolate biscuits.'

'And what do you do at Aisling?'

'I have no idea yet,' he said. 'They've told me to write me own job description.'

He smiled without showing me his teeth, and I read in the expression a lack of ease with the prospect of that kind of freedom. 'Do you have share options?' he asked. I nodded my head. 'Me too. They're worth a fecking fortune. But I can't trade them in for three years. Do you think the company will last that long?'

'I think it will,' I said.

'It's a good company, isn't it?'

'The best I've worked for.'

'It's going to last, right?'

'Can't see it not lasting,' I said.

'I've given myself a year,' he said. 'I'm on a sabbatical, you see. I told the wife that if things didn't work out I could always go back.'

'Things'll work out,' I said. Did I believe it myself? I suppose I did, mostly. That was new.

*

The following morning we were woken at half-eight and, after breakfast, asked to gather in the meeting room for a session on personal development. As we filed in, the light of the mounting sun filled the room with a colour like candied orange peel; for a moment I felt as if I had entered a room painted this colour and wondered if Larry hadn't, indeed, turned the room into some kind of colour-therapy sauna, orange for better performance, that kind of thing, but then I remembered that we'd been in this room the previous day and that the walls were painted white.

As my eyes adjusted to the brightness, I saw Aengus standing, in silhouette, at the head of the room. On the plane I told Larry that my disagreement with Aengus had stemmed from a philosophical difference of opinion, but the truth was that I disliked him and had done so from almost as soon as he'd introduced himself to us, yet I couldn't at first have told you why. But as he moved from the stance he had taken up and began to address us, my brain caught up with my peptides and I understood that what I disliked was exactly his tendency to adopt such poses and all that went with them: that is, the insincere smile, and the exaggerated body movements, and the calculated shifts in intonation and syntax: it was worse than smooth—it was just cheap showmanship, and utterly unconvincing.

I slouched in my seat and directed my gaze not at him or the whiteboard on which he wrote notes but out the window, only half listening as he explained how the map was the territory and how, in order to excel, we had to reorient our maps according to the models provided by experts in fields as diverse as management, teaching, parenting, 'even ... ah ... *intimate relations*'.

He paused before pronouncing this final item, and the conspiratorial beat made everyone laugh.

'I'm serious,' he said. 'Forget the Kama Sutra. What you need when you want to improve your sex-life is to find some couple having mind-blowing sex and—preferably with their consent;

I'm not advocating anything illegal here—take notes. You'd be surprised at how much you'd learn.'

There was more laughter and he smiled with pleasure; it made me want to fucking pound him.

'Cheap gags about sex almost always get a laugh,' he said. 'I modelled that on the great comedians.'

He sipped a glass of water, then went on, 'But the thing you'll find about the people you choose to model is that very often—most of the time, in fact—they'll be completely unconscious of the elements that constitute their excellence. Modelling someone, then, is mostly a process of uncovering the unconscious pattern of their excellence.'

He took another sip, and raked his gaze across the room. It settled on me.

'You don't seem convinced,' he said lightly, a joke: as if anyone could fail to be convinced by him.

And I realise that what I should have said was something insipid, something like, 'No, I am convinced,' something that wouldn't get me into trouble, but what I actually said was—though I'm still not sure how it slipped so easily by my mental censor, it was like a different part of me was doing the talking—what I said was, 'No, I think it's interesting, but isn't it just a little bit like brainwashing?'

He didn't immediately answer.

'You're familiar with these teachings?' he asked, striving to sound unruffled.

'I've read a few books.' Clipped, not conceding anything.

'Well ...' he said slowly, trying to make it sound as if he wasn't reproaching me, but nonetheless making it clear how wrong he thought I was, 'well, you've obviously misunderstood what they were about.'

I said nothing. I folded my arms and set my smile against him: thin, narrow, obstinate.

*

That was Saturday.

On Sunday afternoon, while we waited for the arrival of the minibus that would bring us back to Dublin, Aengus approached me as I stood looking out of the large window in the library; he asked if I would like to accompany him on a stroll.

'I think we got off to a bad start yesterday,' he said, then added, when I returned his offer with a hard look, 'Clear the air—in the fresh air, as if were.'

It was a weak joke, but the fact that he felt he needed to make it caused me to relax a little.

'Sure,' I said, 'that would be nice.' Lie. I did not want to walk with him, but I knew that I couldn't refuse without causing more trouble for myself.

I was in enough trouble as it was. After our respective opening gambits, I had been prickly, verging on hostile, towards Aengus for the rest of his presentation; he'd been defensive, whilst struggling to appear not to be defensive. The lecture had ended early and without either of us feeling we'd gotten satisfaction. I assumed that Aengus would relay news of my behaviour to Dee and that I'd be reprimanded, or even let go. I tried to justify my behaviour to myself, but couldn't, so then I tried to adopt Tom's attitude (*Fuck it*, I said, *it's only a job*), but a counter-voice told me that I'd never find another job like it, and it was right, though I could see no way to fix the problem without apologising, and that was the one thing I wouldn't do.

Aengus walked out the front door, and I followed him. We stomped off across the driveway, climbed a stile over a wire fence, and set off along a path that coiled through the woods to the west of the house.

'Larry wants to bring in a herd of deer and turn the entire grounds into a deerpark,' said Aengus. 'Did you know that?'

'No,' I said.

'If he can get the locals to agree.'

'I see,' I said.

He had come to a fork in the path. After yesterday's morning session I had spent the afternoon (which had been designated 'free' in advance of an evening of role-playing exercises and workshops based on the morning's presentation) exploring the grounds as a means of not having to talk to anyone. Going left, I knew, we would eventually come to the banks of the river. I didn't know what was to the right.

'I thought what you had to say yesterday was quite interesting,' said Aengus, when I caught up to where he stood at the junction. He looked in both directions, then set off down the right-hand path with a nod of his head and a faint, sub-vocal click that I sensed had settled or at least curtailed an internal debate. The sound of our footfalls on the packed earthen track seemed muffled after the crunch they had made on the gravel; the trees shouldered in more closely about us and the light dropped, dappling, on the shrivelled brown leaves that had already fallen from the trees or were yet poised to fall. There were some scattered stands of birch and hazel and tall Scots pine and a few larch, but mostly it was beech. Long arcades of beech, stretching away all around us, the sunward sides of their ghost-grey boles blistered with the raw red light of the evening.

'It's nice,' he said, talking to me over his shoulder, 'to lead a group in which at least one person has some idea what I'm on about. Refreshing, actually. Usually no one has a clue.'

'I wouldn't consider myself an expert.'

'But you're not a beginner, either.'

'Well.' It was all I could think to say. My feelings of hostility towards this man had resurfaced, sharply; worse, I suspected that he was canny enough to interpret the signals I was emitting, body language, that kind of thing (maybe even fluctuations in my aura—I kept an open mind about stuff like that).

'You know enough to have some reservations about my teaching,' he said.

I smiled inwardly at his understated way of categorising my dissent, and at the affiliated realisation that he was trying very hard to placate me. I had expected to be told to get on board with Larry's vision or to reconsider my future with the company, and I'd steeled myself for that; I had not expected appeasement.

'Like I said, it seems a little like mind control to me.' I said this in a voice as empty of intonation as I could manage. Try to make him believe that this wasn't about him. A statement of fact, not merely an opinion.

'I've heard that before,' he said. 'It's a common misunderstanding.' He stopped walking and turned his head from side to side, as if looking for something, then pivoted on his left foot and beat his way along an overgrown path that led towards a mound that I don't think I would otherwise have spotted. All the while he continued to talk: 'What I'm about is helping you to improve your personal effectiveness in a wide range of circumstances, but especially in interpersonal communications. And sometimes those who employ the techniques I teach are perceived as having an unfair advantage over those who don't.' He reached the mound and stepped through a break in the wall of thorns that crowned the rim to reach a flat space between the trees and the briars. I followed him. I could see nothing from the mound except trees, the corpse-thin branches of their crowns, and, in the distance, the top of an industrial crane, looking particularly literal: a predatory wading bird poised above the town.

'And maybe they do,' he said, continuing, 'but there have been techniques of persuasion around as long as the human race. Used by priests and gurus and shamans and all kinds of tricksters and charlatans and quacks.' He liked this last word, *quacks*, clacking it around his mouth like it was a boiled sweet before going on (without giving me a chance to interrupt), 'At least what I teach isn't couched in the arcane vocabulary of an occult elite. Everything I teach is in the public domain, for anyone to learn. It's very democratic. My techniques can be used by *all* the participants in a transaction: the person who is being persuaded can as easily use my techniques as the person who is doing the persuading. In fact, I rather wish that this is how all transactions were carried out. It would ensure more honesty and plain-speaking in communication, both business and personal, than we are used to.

'*Because*, and this is the point I was trying to emphasise yesterday—perhaps I didn't emphasise it enough—*because* what I'm about is improving the life of the practitioner. If what I teach helps him or her achieve more sales then great, that's great. But if it helps them communicate more effectively and intimately with their partner or kids or parents—and especially with themselves—then that's even better. That's my angle. It's all about self-improvement!'

As he talked, I watched the horizon inhaling the last draughts of the day's light. The silhouettes of the farthest trees were dissolving into one dark uniformity, and thick, cold tentacles of wind were sloughing across the mound. I sucked my elbows into my side and folded my arms against the chill. There was a sudden raucous babble of chit-chat from rooks nestled in the boughs around us.

'You're still not convinced,' he said over the noise of the birds, correctly interpreting my lack of a response.

'It's not about being convinced,' I said. 'I'm sure that you mean everything you say.'

'But ...' he prompted, after I stalled again.

'But, frankly, it feels like a betrayal.'

'A betrayal?' He sounded amused.

'Yes: a betrayal,' I said. It was not the word I had intended to use but now that I had said it I knew it was the only word that suited. Betrayed by whom? What I wanted to say was *This is not what Larry is about* but the prudent aspect of my personality decided instead to speak in universals, saying,

'It seems to me as if what you teach was developed to help people liberate themselves from their limitations, not to help salesmen flog their samples more effectively.

'And what's more,' I added, remembering something else I had wanted to say, and suddenly feeling as gauche as a teenager in an Aldous Huxley novel, but unable to help myself, 'that breathing exercise you had us do at the end of the class, well I've done a little yoga and I know that that's a technique Indian mystics use as a prelude to meditation.'

Another of Larry's principles was that everyone needed to speak their truth. I had assumed by this that the speaking followed the truth, but it now occurred to me that truth could be understood through the very process of trying to verbalise it.

'Sadhus,' he said.

'Sorry?'

'Indian mystics. They call themselves sadhus.'

'Whatever they called themselves they certainly didn't intend their methods to be used by businessmen to calm themselves before important meetings.'

'Well, that's certainly an interesting perspective,' he said after only a slight pause, 'but I'm not sure I share your sense of a rigid division between the commercial and the spiritual. And, anyway, the idea of a conflict between wealth and enlightenment is a very Western indulgence. Correct me if I'm wrong, but wasn't it the Hindus who said that a man was obliged to achieve material success before he could retire to the forest and a life of contemplation?'

'The householder stage,' I stated, determined to let him know that I knew as much about this as he did. 'But that only proves that they didn't make material success the sole measure of a person's worth.'

'And neither do I,' he said, 'and neither does Essentia and neither does Aisling. That's the whole point of this weekend, Eoin. I'm here to convince you that the company you've joined is interested in more than mere material success, for itself or for its employees. Material success has its place, sure, which explains the generous salary you're being paid. But you're right: there's more to life than making money and there's certainly more to life that simply working *for* money. If your job doesn't mean *something* then what's the point of getting up in the morning? You might as well be on the dole or sweeping the streets. A business has to have a mission, a *vision*.

'I think you realise this, Eoin, and forgive me if this seems too familiar, but I sense that you are someone looking for *meaning*. Am I right?'

He wasn't making it any easier for me to like him: he must have been around the same age as me, maybe even younger, but I felt inferior to him, he seemed to reside so lightly in his body, and I seemed so heavy in mine, and, besides, it was hard to trust someone who italicised their speech so much, and I detested being catalogued so glibly, but the cold and the effort of my expositions had drained me: I could only nod.

'That's great,' he said, with something approaching relief. 'Great. Larry'll be pleased.'

*

'You made quite an impression on Aengus, you know,' said Larry, after I'd finished giving him my account of the induction course.

'Really?' I asked. I was not being modest, or disingenuous. The fact that I had not been confronted about my behaviour that weekend had led me to conclude that Aengus had said nothing to Dee or to Larry, or had given them only a neutral report. In my more paranoid moments, I had concluded that Larry *had* been told, but that he had reserved his anger for exactly a situation like this: so that he could reprimand me forcefully and at length. What I had not expected, despite our *rapprochement* on the mound, was to be informed that Aengus had actually praised me.

'Yes. He said that he thought that you had an affinity for what we're trying to do, but also a critical eye, a knack for hard appraisal, as he put it.'

'Did he really say that?' I wondered if perhaps he'd gotten me confused with someone else or had encountered the ghost of my better nature after we'd parted.

'He really said that. He also said that you had your reservations.'

'Well,' I said vaguely, hoping that I'd have to say no more.

'Go on,' he urged: 'be honest.'

'Larry,' I said, still trying to deflect him, 'I thought that what I said had gotten me into trouble with Aengus and I'm pretty sure it's going to get me into trouble with you.'

'Let me say it for you then,' he said. 'If I have it right, you believe that we're somehow tainting these tools of human enlightenment by using them for something as trivial as making money.'

'Something like that,' I mumbled, hearing how ridiculous it sounded when stated in a certain manner.

'I understand,' said Larry. 'Yes, I do: I can understand how you'd think that.' He turned his head to look out the cabin window.

'There were a number of really excellent applicants for your position,' he continued, quietly but clearly. 'Do you know what swung it for you? I mean, your CV was impressive and you interviewed very well, but do you know what made you stand out for me?'

He was looking at me again.

I shook my head.

'The samples of writing you submitted to us really spoke to me.'

'Did they?' I asked. I had included, with my application, a copy of the one 'Pendulum' article that had been published on *Wake.com*, as well as those few parts of the novel I had actually managed to complete.

'They really did. I recognised a kindred spirit in them. Tell me, Eoin, why do you write?'

This was one of my most frequently asked questions, but one to which I did not have a good answer. Or, rather, I did have an answer, but those to which I'd offered it had never understood. It's a compulsion, I'd tell them: I feel compelled to write—I don't have any better explanation than that; if I wasn't writing I'd be a drug addict, I'd add, only half-joking, but Larry wouldn't want to hear that, so I said, 'To leave something behind, I suppose.'

'Yes,' he said eagerly. 'Yes, that's it: you want to create something, something that will last beyond you.'

'That would be nice,' I admitted.

'You're an artist,' he said with approval, a compliment.

'Not really, Larry,' I said, resisting the urge to laugh. 'I haven't even had anything published yet, nothing worth mentioning.'

'But you have aspirations?'

'Well sure,' I said.

'I'm an artist, too,' he continued, 'in a way. I want to leave something behind, something positive: I want to change the world for the better.'

I nodded at him, as if I agreed with him, but really I was cringing, and not just at what he said—his immodesty, his gumption—but also the way he was saying it, with such sincerity, as if there could be no other possible explanation for the way things were except Larry's explanation. And yet his earnestness was beginning to work on me. Somewhere in my gut, just beyond the comprehending reach of my consciousness, I sensed an emotion being loosened, released, unbound; with each breath it siphoned itself a little higher up into my chest.

'You can turn your recorder on again,' he said, pointing to my dictaphone.

'It's on,' I said.

He meditated for a moment. 'If you want to change the world,' he said, 'what options do you have? Art? With all due respect, art never changed anything.'

' "Poetry makes nothing happen",' I whispered.

'What was that?'

' "Poetry makes nothing happen",' I repeated more clearly.

'Who wrote that?'

'Auden,' I said.

'He was English, wasn't he?'

'Very English.'

'Well, we won't hold that against him, because he knew what he was talking about. The thing is that politics isn't much better. Where it has sought to change the world it has only managed to turn it into a concentration camp. I did that whole anti-business, anti-corporate, anti-capitalist thing when I was a student, you know. You'd find me most Saturday mornings at the top of Grafton Street trying to flog copies of the *Socialist Worker*.

'No, really,' he insisted when he saw the look on my face. 'I'm not pulling your leg.'

'What changed your mind?'

'I went to Russia before the collapse of communism,' he said. 'It was just so dreary, Eoin; dreary and drab and hopeless. And it's the same in Cuba and Vietnam and Laos, even China, all those countries where state socialism still exists. And don't be under any illusions that there's not a single person in any of those countries who wouldn't love to live in America, or at least live like an American, wouldn't love to be a wealthy capitalist, wouldn't want their children to grow up to be entrepreneurs.' Another pause. 'Look, capitalism is few people's idea of Utopia, but it's better than the alternatives, that's all I'm saying. And it certainly offers a better chance for someone to make a real difference than any other system of government we've ever had.

'I'm a creator, Eoin,' he said with feeling. 'They say that if you change yourself, the world will change to accommodate you. And if this is true—and I believe it is—then my idea is that if I change the way my company does business then maybe the world will change the way *it* does business. And not just change that benefits the investors and management, but the workers too. We all have to work for a living; we might as well try to create a world where we *enjoy* working for a living, where our job contributes something to our lives rather than being something that robs us of our time, and a place where we can make a difference, not just in our own lives, but in the lives of others, in the life of the community. Businessmen are the new revolutionaries.'

He stopped, and directed such a frank and wide-eyed look at me that I thought he was trying to hypnotise me into believing him. It was unnerving, but also vaguely comical. I resisted both the urge to back away from him, and the urge to laugh. 'What do you think?' he asked.

You're bullshitting me, man, is what I thought, *and deluding yourself too*. But my reaction was not only mental or rational. It was also physical: the current that had earlier bubbled up from my belly was now gushing out into my extremities: my toes and palms and the tips of my fingers, even my scalp, were tingling, and I was intensely aware that they were all pulsing to the measure of my heartbeat. And more: the energy was leaking out into the ether. I felt a prickling sensation hovering maybe a centimetre above the skin of my hands, my neck, my face, the crown of my head—as if my body was enclosed in an invisible flickering shell.

What I thought was, *This is what I had wanted to hear*.

And what I said was, 'I think that's inspirational.'

*

Lunch was served soon after that.

'Enough business talk,' he said, instructing me to switch off the dictaphone again: 'I want to hear about you.'

'There's not much to tell,' I demurred.

'That's a terrible admission for a writer to make.'

'I don't do that much writing anymore.'

'Why not?' he asked. It was only a short question, but the manner in which he enunciated it made me feel as if I was being interrogated by a therapist, *This is about you, tell me about you*, and I remembered that Larry had had some training in psychology. How much training?

'I'd rather not talk about it,' I said.

'Sure,' he said, as a stewardess placed our trays before us. 'Sure, I understand.'

'A girl,' I said after the stewardess had moved on.

'A girl?'

'A woman.'

'What was her name?' Same measured, solicitous tone.

'Erin.'

'Where did you meet her?'

'Long story.'

'Tell me,' he said.

'Fine,' I said, relenting, and began by telling him how, all during my college years, and for a while afterwards (even now, in fact, though not as often), I'd regularly found myself invited to Bible meetings by strangers who would start talking to me while I waited at a bus stop or sat reading by myself in a coffee shop. They were all of them perfectly nice—high marks for presentation—but not very original, all following pretty much the same script (I wondered was it written down anywhere, the standard pitch they were meant to give to everyone, spiritual telemarketeers), opening the conversation casually, asking me if I had any family, what I did with myself, where did I live and was Christ present in my life? These encounters became such a regular occurrence that I soon began to recognise the type before they even spoke to me. Their body language gave them away, approaching as they all did with a pronounced deference, humility even, in their posture, projecting an aura of openness that was so guileless that I could not be short with them. So I let them talk, allowing them to extend their invitations, and only then politely refusing, even though it pained me to see them try to conceal the hurt my rejection had caused.

Once, though, out of curiosity perhaps, though more likely out of a desire to spare the inviter's feelings, I accepted an offer and attended a Bible meeting, but only once: I did not return. It wasn't that I'd found the teachings naïve and uncritical—that I had expected. What I hadn't expected was to leave feeling inadequate. Confronted with at least the appearance of other people's faith, I was aware that I believed in nothing, except the possibility of believing: I wanted to possess some of their conviction, their sense of rightness, but knew that I couldn't. So. No going back.

I explained all this to Erin after we'd figured out that the place she'd seen me before had been at that Bible meeting. At that time she'd been a regular attendee, though she'd since lapsed too. Yet she retained a little of the holy innocence that had marked the other bashers I had met, notwithstanding the fact that in her it seemed just a little bit self-conscious, a little bit contrived. I was nonetheless beguiled, and, when she had touched my arm that first night in response to something witty

I'd said, some sad little joke, I convinced myself that I felt a jolt of goodness, yes goodness, surge like static up my arm and into my heart.

The things we believe.

The lies we tell ourselves.

None of us are surprised anymore, I suppose, at these lies. We have in fact come to accept, thank you Freud, that we are always lying to ourselves; that, indeed, our consciousnesses may be no more than one constantly reiterated lie, repeated over and over to distract ourselves from the fact of our subversion to the biological imperative. But still. You hope. You hope that you might be different. You hope that you might be able to sneak a few true words past the diktats of one's genes.

When she was breaking up with me, I told her that I loved her.

'You can't,' she said.

And I suppose she was right, I couldn't have, not in the way she'd wanted, but I'd felt compelled nonetheless to say it.

Larry asked, 'Are you two still together?'

'God, no,' I said.

'What happened?'

'We just weren't compatible,' I said.

'You seeing anyone at the moment?'

'I'm not really in the market.'

'I don't care what market you're shopping in,' he said, 'as long as it's not mine.' He laughed, as if what he'd said was a joke that I ought to get.

I stared at him without comprehension.

'I heard there were some shenanigans at the induction.'

'Shenanigans?'

'People hooking up, that sort of thing.'

'Hooking up?'

'You know what I mean, Eoin.'

'And you don't approve?'

'Didn't Dee mention it to you?'

'Mention what?'

'Eoin, you know that I'm not one for rules'—I nodded; *I know that, Larry*—'but if and when you do go looking for a girlfriend again I'd rather you didn't go looking in the Aisling pool, as it were.'

'Fine,' I said.

'Dee should have mentioned it to you. It's not the kind of thing we broadcast, but my managers are instructed to let their people know exactly where I stand on office romance.'

'She didn't mention a thing.'

'Relationships complicate things, you understand.'

'I understand.'

'Do you?' He looked me up and down, to verify if I meant what I said. 'Good. I hate laying down the law, any law, but I feel very strongly about this.'

'Larry,' I said, 'it's really fine. I'm not really looking anyway.'

'Focused on more important things?' he suggested.

'Something like that,' I said.

*

Larry and I said goodbye to each other in the terminal at JFK. He tried to persuade me to accompany him to the company's apartment in Manhattan but I told him that there didn't really seem much point in that, given that my flight back to Ireland was leaving in less than five hours.

After I received Larry's email about the flight, I went to find

Dee to OK it with her, but she already knew; Larry had cleared it with her first.

'You don't seem too put out,' she said.

'It's New York,' I replied.

'Actually, Eoin, about that: I have some bad news.' She drew her mouth into a grimace, the first time I think I had seen her without a smile since I'd joined Aisling. 'I'm sorry to do this to you, but you'll be flying back the same day.'

'The same day?' I said, unable to stop myself sounding disappointed—I was disappointed: I'd expected that she was going to tell me that the bad news was that I'd have to spend at least a day or two in New York before coming home.

'I know that you would probably have liked to stay for a couple of days'—I raised my eyebrows and rolled my eyes upwards, *What can you do?*—'but Padraig Finn, our CFO, will be coming back with you on the return flight.'

'Am I to interview him too?'

'Yes.'

'And this is the only window he has in his schedule?'

'Afraid so. He's as elusive as Lawrence, and a really difficult man to have an uninterrupted conversation with.'

'She didn't really say that, did she?' asked Tom, when I later that day told him about the conversation.

'Word for word,' I swore.

He tipped back his head, laughing. 'Fucking hell,' he declared, 'but that woman has absolutely no sense of irony.'

'What's up?' I asked, worried.

Tom gave me a look. 'They call him "Basking", y'know.'

'Because of his name?'

'His name?'

'Finn,' I said, making a blade of my right hand and hobbyhorsing it along an imaginary horizon.

'No, you gobshite,' said Tom. 'They call him Basking because to him we're all just little fish swimming in his sea. He'd swallow you up whole and hardly even notice. We're all just food to him.'

'Christ.'

'I tried to interview him once.'

'And ...?'

'And nothing. He chose the first meeting we had together as the perfect time to take a power nap and then when I scheduled our next meeting in a café, he spent the whole time chatting up our waitress. I think he got off with her too, the fucker.'

The thought of flying home with Basking must have been preoccupying me because Larry asked, as we were waiting for his luggage, what was bothering me.

'Just nervous about the flight home.'

'Heard stories about Padraig, have you?'

I shrugged my shoulders.

'Don't worry about Paddy. And look,' he went on, 'when I'm back in Ireland, you're going to follow me around for a few days. Accompany me, that is. Come with me to meetings and presentations, hear the story of Aisling as I tell it. It will help you to write it better.

'Also,' he continued, though he hesitated slightly before proceeding, and afterwards, when I reflected on it, I wondered if he had made the invitation merely to compensate me for the inconvenience of my situation, 'also there's a small group of us in the company who meet on a regular basis to discuss some of the things you and I have been discussing, and I'd like to invite you to join.'

I didn't commit myself to an immediate response. I'd heard

about Larry's group. All the other senior managers were required to supply one-on-one mentoring to their subordinates, but Larry didn't have the time for that, so he compensated by gathering together, every two or three weeks, a group that Tom had dubbed the 'Inner Circle'.

Larry prompted me for a response. 'Well?'

'I'd be delighted,' I said. I *was* delighted. And flattered, too. The invitation appealed to my vanity, but to something else as well. I resolved to lay aside all my reservations and at least for now take a stake in Larry's vision. I felt that I could believe in what he was selling, that it was something I could buy into.

'You don't look so happy,' he said.

'It's nothing,' I said, 'just thinking about the flight home.'

Larry clasped a hand to my shoulder. 'I told you not to worry,' he said: 'Flying with Paddy won't be nearly as awful as some people may have told you.'

*

It was worse.

I occupied myself for four hours in the chain stores and eating halls of the terminal, then waited in front of the Aer Lingus check-in desk with increasing agitation as boarding time approached and Finn didn't show. As they were announcing the close of check-in for our flight, and I was deliberating whether or not to just go ahead without him, a man entered the concourse and walked towards me and although I'd never met Basking or seen his photograph I knew that this was him.

'Cullen?' he asked when he reached me.

I nodded.

'You checked in yet?'

'No sir,' I said.

'We'd better get a fucking move on then,' he said, as if my actions had been the cause of our tardiness.

I had conceived a mental image of Basking as a tall, bulky, blubbery man, but I had conceived incorrectly. He was tall alright, but spare—almost savagely so. And his face had none of the baleen indifference I had expected; on the contrary, I thought it had in it a kind of selachian rapaciousness, more akin to a bull than to a basking shark.

As we were checked through at the executive counter, he asked me why I hadn't checked myself in earlier instead of waiting for him. 'You could be in the executive lounge right now,' he said, 'running up a tab for yourself.'

Larry hadn't mentioned this as an option and I hadn't thought of it on my own initiative but I didn't want to say that so I told him, 'I didn't want to presume.'

'Oh don't be so bloody meek,' he snapped. 'It's one of the perks. If you can't get pissed at the company's expense in the most congested airport in the world, what's the fucking point of working for us?'

I couldn't tell if he was being serious, or if he was baiting me, waiting for my contradiction, *Couldn't possibly do that, sir, wouldn't be right, not on the company tab.* Caught, and confused, the only response I could make was to just stand there and give him the rictal smile of a cur who had been put in his place.

Not the right choice. He was not impressed. He glanced at me with contempt, then flicked his eyes away, around the concourse, over the girl at the desk. Bored. It was obvious that I had been tested and found wanting. I decided that I didn't care about Basking's opinion. And, aware of the bile swilling in my gut, I also decided that I hated him intensely.

'He's a complete fucking prick, isn't he?' said Tom, when I gave him my account of events.

'You sound like you admire him,' I said.

'Without Basking there'd be no Aisling.'

'I don't understand why Larry doesn't get rid of him,' I said, ignoring Tom's comment.

'Because without Basking there'd be no Aisling,' insisted Tom, cutting in before I could elaborate my point.

'That's bullshit.'

'Why is it bullshit?'

'Because Aisling is Larry's company,' I said as if stating a self-evident fact.

'Sometimes, Cullen,' said Tom, after a long pause, 'you are almost unbelievably naïve.'

'I can't believe you're defending that philistine,' I said, stung by the *ad hominem* attack but not yet ready to concede the argument, 'especially after what he did to you.'

'He didn't do anything to me. Nothing that serious. Nothing I wouldn't have done myself. Besides, without that philistine neither of us would have a job.'

'Without Larry we wouldn't have jobs.'

'Listen, Eoin,' he said with practised, weary patience, 'Larry doesn't have a fucking clue about finance. If it wasn't for Basking the company would have gone bankrupt months ago.'

'So he's a good bookkeeper. Big fucking deal.'

'Basking's a businessman. He remembers what Larry seems to have forgotten: how to keep creditors sweet, investors happy, and the revenue commissioners out of your books. Without that kind of cop-on a company doesn't have a chance.'

'A company's nothing without ideas.'

'Everyone and their senile granny can have an idea. It takes something special to turn ideas into profit.'

'It's not just about profit.'

'It's only ever about profit, Eoin,' he said, 'don't let Larry make you believe otherwise. It'll get you into trouble.'

I conceded the argument to Tom, but only because he'd beaten me on points, ding ding, not because he had convinced me of Basking's intrinsic worth. Nothing could have done that. The man had ignored me for most of the rest of the flight home. When I eventually and nervously asked him if he'd like to be interviewed for the brochure, he picked up the in-flight maga-zine, flicked through it, then put it down.

'I'm tired,' he'd said then, leaning his seat back. 'I need a kip. I'll email you everything you need to know.'

He never did. In the end, under pressure from Deirdre to finish the brochure so that we could send it to the printers, I took what Tom had told me and padded it out.

(Source: interview, *The New Irish Entrepreneur*, 15/04/2000)

THE BUDDHA OF IRISH BUSINESS
by William Gibbs

I have been trying to interview Lawrence Cooley, the founder and CEO of Aisling Ltd, for weeks. He's a difficult man to have a conversation with; his schedule, as his assistant keeps pointedly reminding me, is very full.

When I do finally get to talk to him, it's by phone. He's in Aisling's newly opened offices in New York, and I'm in Dublin. Near the end of our chat, he turns the fact of our transatlantic tête-à-tête into a parable about Ireland's changing place in the world.

He pauses for a second after finishing. 'Sorry,' he says, sounding a little abashed. 'Bad habit of mine.'

It's hard to imagine Cooley, 33, having any bad habits. By his own admission a bit of a fitness freak, Cooley jogs every day, lifts weights whenever he can get to a gym, doesn't smoke, and drinks only the occasional glass of red wine. He also finds the time to coach an underage soccer team once a week and meditates for at least half an hour every morning and evening, a practice he credits with providing the basis of his business success. ('I wouldn't be where I am today if I couldn't bloody centre myself,' he jokes.) An ascetic in the hedonistic world of the frequent-flyer executive, it's not surprising that Cooley should be fond of using fables to drive home his arguments. He is famous (perhaps that should be infamous) in Irish business circles for believing that business is about more than turning a profit: it's about changing the world.

'Of course,' he says, when I put

this to him. 'If you only want to make money, going into business might disappoint you. You'd be better off going into crime; it's easier. In fact, if you go into business without some vision of a better world than you're probably little better than a criminal anyway.'

When I put it to him that this could be seen as more than a little insulting to businesspeople in general, and his clients in particular, he tells me that he is 'only joking'. After a pause, he adds, 'Half joking.' I'm not sure if the pause is a rhetorical flourish or a glitch on the line.

Lawrence Cooley was born in Louth in 1967. Educated at a fee-paying secondary school, he subsequently attended Trinity College Dublin, where he took a first-class Bachelor's degree in Mathematics and Philosophy in 1990, and a Master's in Organisational Psychology a year later.

Cooley's career in business was, until the mid-'90s, equally as impressive. Hired straight out of college by one of the big consulting firms, he rose quickly through the ranks and looked destined to make partner at an unfeasibly young age.

In 1995, he took a year's sabbatical to pursue an MBA at Harvard. Returning to Ireland in the summer of 1996, he resumed his old position, but resigned a few months later. Shortly afterwards he founded Aisling Ltd (according to Cooley the name is a reference to a genre of eighteenth-century Irish poetry and translates literally as 'Dream Ltd').

'I had to do it,' he says when I ask what made him quit. 'I felt professionally and personally stifled at my old company. They simply weren't open to new ideas.'

New ideas such as his conviction that he could deliver meaningful growth to financial and banking institutions for less money and in less time than was considered possible. How? By using a holistic business model.

I ask him to define what he means by 'holistic'.

'Holism is actually a very old idea,' he explains. 'Despite what people think, there's nothing new-agey or faddish about it at all. It comes from the Greek word 'holos', which means whole, and it's basically the notion that everything is greater than the sum of its parts. People are greater than the sum of their internal organs, for example, and organisations are greater than the sum of their members – or at least, they should be. They have the potential to be.

'The practice of holism, then, on an individual level, is about making the most of our human potential, while on an organisational level it is about helping businesses, governments and NGOs make the most of their potential.'

I cut in, to protest that this is what every consultancy claims to do for its clients.

'True,' he says, 'but another aspect of holistic practice is understanding that health, in the broadest meaning of that word, can't be achieved unless all the needs and desires of an organism – whether that organism is a person or a company – are met in a balanced way. Modern business, and consultancy in particular, is very unbalanced, focusing on the bottom line to the detriment of everything else, to the detriment of a company's social, environmental, ethical and, yes, even spiritual responsibilities. In the long run that's not sustainable. It breeds resentment, both inside and outside the company, and no company will prosper when it's resented by its staff and customers.'

It may sound idealistic and not a little ridiculous, but Cooley and his team have a reputation for achieving results, especially in the field of IT change management.

'Do we?' he asks when I mention this. 'Good. Getting results for our clients is what we're in business to do. It's true that we measure results in a different way than most consultancies, but we're very upfront about that difference, and it doesn't seem to phase our clients too much. They seem very happy with what we're doing and, in the end, that's all that matters.'

Perhaps that is all that matters. But not everyone in Ireland's blossoming IT sector is smitten with Cooley's methodology – or his beliefs.

One high-ranking industry insider told me that he thought the Aisling CEO was 'a f**king flake' and that his methods and ideas were 'f**king new-age hoodoo voodoo'.

Senior managers at Aisling's current clients were happy, when contacted, to talk of the quality of the work done by Cooley and his company, but were reluctant to endorse his philosophy. At best they said that it was an 'interesting alternative' to conventional business practice.

Even some of Aisling's staff (whom Cooley calls 'co-owners' or, occasionally, 'vision partners') are less than impressed with the way their CEO does things. The majority, it has to be said, expressed no dissatisfaction with the way the company is run, and most were staunchly supportive of Cooley's alternative approach to work (helped, no doubt, by salaries well above industry standards and very generous bonus and share-option schemes).

But some expressed scepticism, and one or two were openly hostile, when asked what they thought of Cooley's approach. One even went so far as to call Cooley a 'fraud'. None, however, wanted to go on the record with their comments.

Cooley himself is not overly concerned with such criticism. He believes his fellow CEOs and senior executives will just have to get used to his way of doing business.

'In five or ten years,' he claims, 'this is the way we'll all be working. The world is changing. People are going to have to let go of their prejudices and just deal with it.'

And his internal critics?

'Maybe it's the case that I haven't sold these changes as best I could. That's something I obviously need to work harder at. But there are always people who resist change, regardless of how benign or benevolent it is. Look, we're not a prison, and we're not detaining these people against their will. If they don't agree with what we're doing, they are free to go. But if they decide to stay, they'll have to decide to give my ideas a chance. If they don't, they're just going to get in the way of our growth, and that's just not acceptable.'

The Buddha of Irish business displaying a little bit of steel – though you wonder whether by 'growth' he means increased profit or the continued self-development of his staff. In Lawrence Cooley's world, of course, the two are not mutually exclusive.

4. People:
Aisling's Greatest Asset

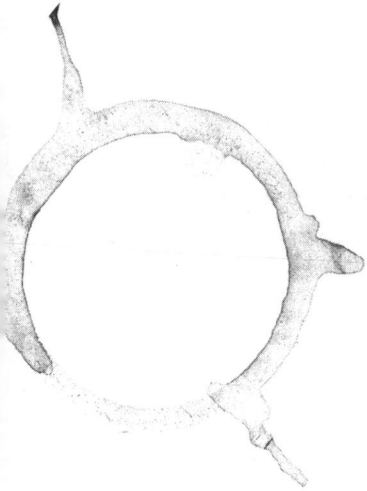

During the first three months of 2000, Tom was summoned regularly from his desk in order to give his input into ongoing projects at various client-sites. I missed him. We had become friends, despite the fact that he remained largely as he had first presented himself to me: prickly and opinionated, aggressively inquisitive and harshly, often unjustly, judgemental. Yet I had come to admire and even value these traits. And I had also come to value his straightness, and his confidence, and even his unexpected outbursts of equanimity.

I was also somewhat in awe of his capabilities. He was if not a prodigy then certainly damn close, and polymatically so—during the early course of our acquaintance, I discovered that Tom had in his teens won a couple of Feis Ceoil awards for his violin playing, been a finalist in the Young Scientist competition, captained his school's rugby team, made it to the All Ireland finals of the university debating championships, and graduated from college with a first-class honours degree. But he was so modest regarding his accomplishments that I couldn't begrudge them to him. He didn't, as others might have, conspicuously allude to his achievements in conversation; they just sometimes happened to arise and, when they did, were stated matter-of-factly, without any pretension. He did not consider his achievements remarkable. Nor did he consider himself as being in any way extraordinary. He was not uniquely talented, he maintained, it was just that he applied himself, had drive. Failure, he argued, could not be explained away by genetics; there were no geniuses or dullards in his world, just people who worked hard and people who didn't work at all—or worked only half-heartedly.

I suspected that he thought I was one of this latter breed, but that I might also, under his guidance, unfetter myself of the shackles of my sloth and accomplish something remarkable. Perhaps this is why I liked him, despite everything—he saw in me a potential that I did not myself perceive. And perhaps it's why he insisted we continue to meet (though for lunch, once or twice a week, rather than for pints in the evening): so that he could continue to monitor the results of his investment of time in me.

But whereas before Christmas we would have talked about nothing except work, now we talked about everything but, and whenever I moved to bring it up Tom said he was tired of the topic; it simply wasn't worth the aggro, especially since we held such differing opinions on Larry and his project. Which is why it wasn't until two or three months later that I mentioned to him that I'd been invited to join Larry's mentoring group.

'I heard that had been put on hold,' he said, sounding dubious.

'It was,' I said. 'I joined in November.'

'Really? I didn't hear that, and I usually hear about these things.'

'Maybe people didn't think it was that big a deal.'

'Maybe,' he said. 'Tell me one thing.'

'Sure.'

'How did you swing it? How did you, Mr Eoin-fucking-Cullen, get yourself invited into Larry's little cabal?' He chuckled as he asked the question but, beneath the laughter, I thought I sensed intimations of jealously. Jealously was not an emotion I would have thought Tom capable of.

'I don't know,' I said, trying to make it sound unimportant. I had started the conversation to make a point, but now I felt that it was not a point that I should belabour.

'Of course you know,' he insisted. 'Don't give me that modesty bullshit.'

'I suppose I raised some questions,' I said.

'What kind of questions? I "raised questions" and all I got was grief.'

'Just questions,' I said. I thought Tom was being uncharacteristically petty; I could be petty too.

'What kind of questions did you ask?' he asked again.

'Jesus, you're being a bit insistent, Tom,' I said.

'I'm just curious,' he said. Conciliatory. 'Indulge my curiosity. What kind of questions did you ask?'

I looked away from him and reconstructed in my mind's eye the sequence of events in Aengus's presentation and the kind of questions I had asked.

'Aengus was talking,' I said, my eyes closed, 'about how we should strive for full disclosure in our interpersonal communications, and I guess I may have mentioned Derrida and Foucault and that whole French theory of the indeterminacy of signs.'

I opened my eyes.

Tom was scowling.

'Whatever the fuck that means,' he said, although I got the impression that he knew well what it meant.

I did not elaborate. I waited for Tom to speak. Ours was an unequal relationship. I understood that. Tom was superior to me, and I acquiesced to that, had tacitly given him the power to dictate the boundaries of our association, never suspecting that I might ever possess even a little influence over it myself. But the silence that had dropped into place between us, and the manner in which Tom had turned his body sideways to mine and started to fiddle with the salt-and-pepper cellars, suggested that a little of the power in the relationship had, temporarily at least, been diverted to me.

'So how did that Aengus guy respond to your observations?' he asked in a voice that was a nearly flawless imitation of his habitually blunt and incurious tone. Nearly, but not quite.

'He told me that all those philosophers were just frustrated mystics, which I couldn't argue with,' I said, teasing.

'He didn't fucking say that,' said Tom, clearly not in the mood for pissing around.

'No,' I conceded, 'he didn't really say that. He didn't really say anything, actually, nothing specific, nothing that I can remember.'

'And yet Larry invited you to join his little mentoring group.'

'He must have seen something in that personality test they made us do.'

'Hm.' He didn't sound impressed.

'Maybe Larry made a mistake,' I said with calculated deprecation. 'Maybe he really meant to choose you.'

'Bollocks,' said Tom. 'I was in the group already. Before you joined.'

'You left?'

'I was asked to leave.'

I didn't sense any advantage would accrue to me if I commented, so I remained silent, as did Tom, though when it became a little uncomfortable and I suggested that we should maybe get the bill, Tom asked, 'You've fucking fallen for it, haven't you?'

'Fallen for what?'

'Larry's whole guru thing. I fucking knew you would, Eoin. He's a fraud, a fucking fraud. A fucking hypocrite too.'

There was disappointment in Tom's words; disappointment with me. But however much I might have desired Tom's approbation, I desired Larry's more.

'Larry's not a fraud,' I said. 'He believes in what he's doing.'

'Maybe that's even worse,' said Tom, 'thinking that he can change the world. You can't fucking change the world, and you certainly can't change other people. You can't even change yourself. Anyone who thinks otherwise is a fool.'

I wanted to tell him that Larry was no fool but I knew it wouldn't get a hearing so I decided instead to change my angle of attack. 'You take it awful fucking personally,' I said.

'Because it's just such bullshit,' he said.

'There has to be more to it than that,' I countered, detecting behind his unreasonableness a weakness I had not previously suspected. 'You get very worked up about it.'

'Don't fucking start psychoanalyzing me, you,' he said. 'I had enough of that from my parents.'

'Psychologists?'

'Teachers,' he said, adding, when he saw my bemused look, 'progressive teachers. They didn't believe in punishment; they believed in lessons. Life lessons. Everything was a lesson to them. When I misbehaved, that was a lesson. Maybe I was crying out for attention or perhaps I wanted more affection or there might even have been some underlying issue that I was ignoring or sublimating, choosing instead to express it through aberrant behaviour. That's what they talked like. I was never bold, you understand: I was behaving aberrantly.'

'What would they do to you if you were … being aberrant?'

'What would they do? They'd fucking sit me down, and tell me that I had to own the damage that I had caused, had to take responsibility for my behaviour. And it worked: Christ, the thought of having to endure another one of their lectures about personal responsibility was probably a more effective deterrent than the thought of a thrashing. And all in the same measured voice: de duh, de duh, de duh de duh de duh. It was all so very fucking reasonable. If I ever have children—and it's very unlikely that I will, but if I do—I'm going to make sure they're given a good thumping every now and then. I think it does you good to hate your parents.'

'Do you hate your parents?'

'What kind of question is that?'

'The kind of question you'd ask.'

He looked at me and curled his lips into an almost-smile, as if to say, *There might yet be some hope for you.*

'Do I hate my parents?' He tilted back his head and stared at the ceiling while he considered the idea. 'Let's put it this way,' he said, bringing his gaze back to my level, 'I was glad when they sent me away to boarding school; it meant I could get some real fucking discipline for a change.'

I looked at him, appraising the degree of his sincerity.

'Joking,' he said. 'Listen, do you have any idea what this meeting is about?'

The meeting he was referring to was the Aisling Staff Conference that Larry had announced unexpectedly only the week before; we were due to attend directly after lunch. The way Tom had asked his question caused some synapse in my head to briefly flare. It was, evidently, the prospect of the meeting that had put him in such a foul mood. I should have known.

'No idea at all.'

'You think it's about that article that was published in *The NIE*? I heard that Larry got really fucking pissed about it.'

'I didn't hear that.'

'And you claim to work in Communications.'

'If there was anything to hear I'd have heard it.'

'How can you be sure?'

'Dee would have said something.'

'Have you talked to him recently though?'

'Talked to who? To Larry?'

'No, to the Pope. Have you talked to the Pope recently?'

I stared at him for a moment, perplexed, before he said, 'Of course to Larry. Who the hell else do you think I meant?'

'Not for three or four weeks,' I said with as much calm as I could marshal. 'Not since he cancelled the mentoring sessions.'

'Lucky you.'

No, not lucky me, is what I wanted to say, but I only smiled in response to his bait, let him read into that what he liked.

Before work commitments had forced him into an indefinite suspension, Larry met with his group at the same time every second Saturday in a room in a hotel just off Merrion Square; each meeting generally lasted until lunch and consisted of a lecture delivered by Larry, followed by questions and answers. (If he was available on the intervening weekends, he brought us out to the Wicklow Mountains to walk or climb or paddle—to give his throat a break, he said, as well as to build a sense of community outside the office.) Ironically, I might initially have concurred with Tom's assessment of these sessions, as my first one hadn't begun too promisingly. When I arrived—fifteen minutes early and a little nervous—the only person in the room I recognised was Fintan O'Connor. I approached him to say good morning. He was standing at a side counter with a plate in his hand.

'Eoin,' he said, turning in response to my greeting, 'I didn't know you'd been fast-tracked into the big boys' club, too.'

'No more than yourself,' I said.

'It gets better,' he said. 'I'm head of me own department now.'

'Congratulations,' I said. 'When did that happen?'

'Only heard about it yesterday. I'm telling you, this would never have happened in me old place, not this fast anyway: it would have taken at least another five years and loads of lick-arsing to get where I am now with Aisling.'

'Your wife will be happy,' I said.

'She'll never be happy,' he laughed, 'not until I'm running the fecking place.' He nodded his head at the food that was arrayed on the counter. 'Tempting selection, isn't it?'

'It sure is,' I said, trying to sound enthusiastic about the bottles of still and sparkling mineral water, the cartons of juice, the plain butter biscuits and the fresh fruit on the counter.

'I hear it's brain food,' he said. 'Keeps your blood sugar up for improved concentration and all that. You are what you eat, don't you know.'

'Where's the tea and coffee?' I asked.

'There is no tea or coffee,' said a voice from behind us. Larry's voice. I turned my head to find him standing behind us; O'Connor turned his head, too.

'Jesus, Larry,' I said, 'how long have you been there?'

'Just arrived,' he said.

'So you don't know who hid the tea and coffee then?' asked O'Connor, trying, but failing, to slide the quip lightly from his tongue; it fell heavily between the three of us. I sensed his embarrassment, and Larry must have too because what came next was uttered in a bantering manner:

'No one hid them,' he said, patting O'Connor on the shoulder. 'It's just that I don't allow people to drink caffeine during the meeting. It disturbs your equilibrium. Makes it difficult to stay centred.'

With any group I have ever joined (and I've joined plenty — meditation groups, book clubs, yoga classes, that Bible meeting) it has typically taken me until a gathering has gotten underway to appreciate that I do not belong there, temperamentally or theologically. But even before this one had started, Larry's little sermon—however lightly delivered—caused a bubble of disillusionment to inflate within me. In my head, all I heard was what Tom would have said.

The surface tension of this bubble of doubt was further corroded when Larry called the meeting to order and explained that before he began he was going to conduct a short 'mood check-in'.

'This is basically,' he said for the benefit of myself and Fintan, 'where we take a few moments to clear our minds and put aside any negative thoughts that might interfere with what we're trying to accomplish here.'

This exercise seemed to be the customary starting-point of the meeting as the other attendees had already closed their eyes and assumed meditative poses: backs straight, feet firm on the floor, hands resting palms-down on their knees or folded lama-like in their laps. I did likewise, despite my scepticism, and listened as Larry urged us to concentrate on our breathing and on each exhalation to release a little more of the negativity within us.

'How was that, Fintan?' he asked when we were done. 'Eoin?'

'Good,' said Fintan.

'Good,' I said as well. And I meant it. It had been good: surprisingly so. I felt, in fact, emptied of all doubt and disbelief; they were outside of me, dissipating into the ether, and it was a revelation. If there was a moment when it could be said that I joined Larry's cause—became, however briefly, an acolyte—it was that moment. The scepticism came back eventually. It always does. Sometimes not even the breathing could dispel it. But attending Larry's meetings and going on those excursions out of the city with him made me feel important; made me, for a while, feel part of something new and interesting.

For a while.

I later learned from Dee that Larry had, before I'd joined the company, tried to convince all his managers to begin every meeting they conducted with a similar breathing exercise, but the idea had found favour with only a few and had been quietly phased out, although Larry had promised to try to introduce it again—when the time was right.

Tom suspected, indeed, that Larry had convened 'this get-together just so that he can foist on us some new scheme he's dreamt up for our fucking self-improvement'.

'Would that be so bad?'

Tom gave me a scornful look. 'We'll just ignore it anyway,' he said, 'whatever it is—until the Maharishi drops it. Like we always do.'

I got the impression that he wanted to say something further, but all he did say, after we'd paid the bill, was, 'Well, let's get to this bloody thing.'

*

The conference was being held in the largest conference room in the Merriman Hotel—a large, windowless space one flight of stairs down from the reception area. When we arrived, Tom nudged me and directed my attention to the message being projected from a laptop onto a large white screen at the end of the room, behind the podium. AISLING STAFF CONFERENCE 2000: A NEW FUTURE FOR AISLING, it proclaimed, as it dissolved and reconstituted itself, then flipped and tumbled across the screen, before dissolving again. I glanced at Tom who flicked his eyes towards the ceiling: *What did I fucking tell you?*

I made my way to the second row of chairs from the podium; I expected that Tom would follow me, but when I took my seat I saw that he had gone to have a word with a group of men and women I didn't recognise. I thought they looked like programmers. They were dressed like programmers. They stood at the back of the room, between the two sets of doors leading into the suite, and the way they stood—their body language, knowing they had to be there, put in an appearance for the sake of appearances, but couldn't wait to get away—made me think of men loitering in the narthex of the church during Sunday Mass.

Tom was at the centre of the group. He was talking to them with spirit. They were, I supposed, people he had met while client-site yet I would never have suspected that he could have known so many, nor that he could be as popular with them as he so obviously was. He had certainly never displayed to me any tendency to cultivate that kind of popularity. He had also never seemed to like being with a crowd, rarely tagging along, for instance, when the office had gone for pints; he would at most have put in an appearance for one or two rounds, and then made his excuses.

As the room filled up, Tom didn't give any indication that he would break off from this group, but I held a place for him as long as I could, even after it was clear that there wouldn't be a seat for every member of staff, arriving, as they were, from every one of Aisling's sites. Eventually a woman asked me if the chair beside me was free and I said of course it was, retrieving the jacket I had draped there and laying it across my lap. She sat down. I smiled politely at her. She smiled back. We didn't say anything to each other.

I looked about the room. It was designated, according to the brass plaque beside the entrance doors, as 'The Poets' Suite'. The decorators had laid down a beige carpet and hung on the walls—painted a shade of sensible, corporate blue—gilt-framed portraits of Ireland's poets, as well as prints of their most famous poems, as if the room was a gallery and we were attending an exhibition of bardic verse.

I had just decided to get up to see which poems were on display when Larry and the management team entered through a door at the back of the room. The managers (including Basking and Deirdre, Fintan O'Connor, and even Aengus) took their places on the chairs arranged for them on the podium, while Larry walked to the lip and looked out at us.

He seemed confident enough, even though I knew that he did not like speaking in public. Hated it, actually. Oh, sure, he was fine in front of a small group—more than fine, he was dynamic and dominant—but in front of crowds his poise disintegrated. I wouldn't have believed it possible either, would have dismissed the idea as nonsense, *Not Larry*, if I hadn't happened to be with him just before he'd been due to deliver a speech (which I had helped to write) to an audience of maybe five or six hundred people at a conference about opportunities in the New Economy.

We had been escorted to the wings of the stage to await Larry's signal to go on. I remember that I did not pay much attention to Larry, figuring that he was fine, but concentrated instead on what the speaker presently on stage was saying, then thought I ought to at least seem interested, and turned to Larry to ask if he was ready.

There had been a remarkable transformation in his appearance since we'd taken our places. Bulbous beads of sweat had blossomed on his forehead and neck, soaking the collar of his shirt and blotching his cheeks with red algoid forms. His shoulders were hunched. He was shivering as if he was cold. And his hands were shaking. My eyes, attracted by this motion, dropped down, and when they elevated themselves again I found Larry staring at me, with a look in his eyes of mingled shame and cravenness.

'I can't do this,' he said. 'I can't go out there.'

I looked mutely at him. I was conflicted. I was not used to

seeing a man in whom I had placed so much trust demean himself before me and I could not decide whether I ought to persuade him to take his place on the stage, or respect his wishes and lead him back to the speakers' hospitality area.

Or should I let him decide for himself what to do, without making myself an accomplice, one way or the other? A part of me (I won't quantify how large it was, but large enough, larger than I would have suspected) was furiously canvassing me to do nothing, to let Larry act as he would, to see how he dealt with the pressure, maybe see him crumble, what a sight that would be, the great man brought low, et cetera, et cetera.

But that would have been too cruel. I decided to intervene.

'You'll be fine,' I told him. What else to say? What words would encourage him? 'You'll be fine,' I repeated. I could think of nothing else to say.

'Where's Deirdre?' he asked.

Dee had been due to attend the conference, but had earlier phoned me on my mobile to let me know that her train had been delayed and that she'd be late, if she made it at all. I relayed this information to Larry.

'Call her for me,' he demanded, sounding a little more like his usual, baseline self. I dialled Dee's number on my phone and handed it to him, a little annoyed that he hadn't thought to use his own.

'Hi, it's me,' he said. 'No, Larry. I'm just about to go on.'

Pause. I could hear her voice—the timbre, the rhythm, the lilt—but could not tell what she was saying.

'Yeah, a little,' he said ruefully. 'You know how I get before I do one of these things.'

She probably then said something like, *Listen to me, Lawrence*, because that's what he did for the next several minutes, just listened. I still couldn't hear her properly, but I figured that she was encouraging him to breathe, because he began to draw long, deep breaths into his chest, and held them there, and then released them slowly. It seemed to restore his confidence, or at least the appearance of confidence. When he was introduced, he strode onto the stage and gave a speech that was, if not perfect, than at least more than adequate.

'What did you say to him?' I asked Deirdre, when she arrived during the closing stages of his performance.

'I told him I'd be here to see the end of his speech, and that I'd kick his ass if he fucked it up.'

'You didn't.'

'You sometimes need to take a firm line with Lawrence, or he'd completely fall apart. But don't let him know I told you that.'

'Told me what?' I asked with faux-gaucheness.

She smiled and touched my arm.

I wondered if a similar drama had been acted out before he'd walked onto the podium this afternoon. I looked at Dee, who was looking at Larry as he tinkered with the laptop; she sensed my regard and winked at me. I smiled back at her, then looked again at Larry, who was ready to begin.

The screensaver disappeared and was replaced with a black blankness.

'Hello everyone,' said Larry. 'Thank you for coming. I know this is a busy time of year for everybody so I appreciate the effort you've made to get here today.'

This was a false sentiment. Larry was making it sound as if attendance at the meeting had been a matter of personal choice even though his circular had made it plain that attendance was mandatory. If Larry had intended his salutation to be a joke then it had fallen flat: no one laughed, not even anyone on the management team. If, on the other hand, he had hoped to put us at our ease, this too seemed to have failed. There was a tension in the room—the tension of the potentially unemployed.

I think it's fair to say that whenever the employees of a company are called together for an unscheduled meeting about the company's future they tend—however well the company appears to be doing—to think *restructuring*, which usually means *job losses*.

Tom had said as much as we'd walked from the restaurant to the hotel.

'Whatever this is about,' he'd said, 'I bet that some people are going to lose their jobs.'

'That's rubbish,' I'd replied. 'The company's doing great.'

'I'm not so sure about that,' Tom had said sceptically, and I must admit that I suddenly shared his scepticism. Larry's clumsy opening seemed like the prelude to bad news.

'You are probably wondering why I called you here,' he continued. 'The reasons are threefold. First, I'd like to thank everyone for their hard work during the past twelve months. It's been a good year for Aisling.' There was a small smattering of applause, but Larry signalled that he had more to say. 'It's been a good year for Aisling, and the management team and I are keen to show our appreciation.' Dramatic pause. 'So you'll all be receiving bonuses in your next pay cheque.'

The applause rekindled and spread to the whole room. It lasted until Larry again signalled for silence.

'Second, I'd like to announce that our new conference and corporate retreat centre is now officially open for business. I know some of you have already been there as part of the induction course, but the centre is now open to everyone in Aisling. If you need to get away for a weekend to decompress, or would like to take your team away for a brainstorming session or a project-review meeting, then talk to Declan, our General Manager, who'll be happy to accommodate you. I'd also like to take this opportunity to thank Declan for taking responsibility for the Kilcoyle project and for seeing it so conscientiously through to completion.'

Larry turned to Declan, who was seated amid the other managers, and began to clap. The applause was picked up by us again, but in a more polite and less sustained manner than before.

'Finally,' he said, when this applause had died away, then paused to take a sip of water, 'finally, while this year has been a good one for the company, it has also been an expensive year, and we need to discuss ways of reducing our costs.'

Job losses. Fuck. It's what I thought. I'm sure it's what everyone thought. Larry must have thought so too, because he added: 'Now I'm not talking about job losses, at least not yet. But we are living beyond our means, and we will soon have to let people go unless we can cut some costs.'

This was a shock to me. I had heard nothing of this. I wondered if Tom had known. He probably had. He always seemed to know these things. I resisted the urge to glance over my shoulder to see his reaction, though I suspected that it would most likely be smug. 'It'll be interesting to see how the auld hippie handles firing people,' he'd said as we'd walked up. 'Though he'll never do anything as old-fashioned as laying people off. He'll probably insist that he's merely redirecting their careers out of the company, or some other fucking corporate New Speak like that.'

'Now I know this will be a shock to you,' said Larry. 'It was a shock to me when I saw the figures, but I'd like to assure you—and state very firmly for the record—that this is not a sign of our failure, but of our growing faster than we had expected or made provision for.'

He stopped talking long enough for this thought to percolate through us, then resumed. 'Now, the management team and I have been discussing ways of reducing our costs, and I'm going to go through them one by one, so that you'll understand where we're coming from and that we're not being arbitrary.'

He fiddled for a moment with the laptop and the blank screen was replaced by a PowerPoint™ slide. REDUCING OUR COSTS, it read. Larry pressed the Return button and, underneath this heading, a new legend appeared: 1. BUSINESS LUNCHES.

I sensed the woman sitting beside me shift in her chair. I glanced at her. She caught my look, then flicked her eyes at Larry, arching her brows. In sympathy, I shrugged my head towards my left shoulder and smiled. I understood. We were in this together, me and her and everyone else around us, in this against them up there, and that disturbed me: I had never before felt so outside of Larry's orbit, so menial, so like just another minion in his service.

'The first provision we propose to introduce,' he was saying, 'is a ban on business lunches. In future, you won't be able to charge a lunch to the company unless you're entertaining a client.'

'Why are you mentioning this to us?' asked a voice from the back of the room. Many heads, including mine, turned in the direction of the voice: Tom, of course. He had a look of hard, brittle belligerence on his face.

I turned back in time to see Larry indulgently smiling.

'Because,' he said, 'I'm explaining a change in company policy to you.'

'It's not a change in policy that has any impact on me,' said Tom. 'It's not a change in policy that has any impact on ninety-five per cent of the people in this room. We don't charge lunch to the company. The people you need to be talking to are sitting behind you, in the high chairs. Why don't you address this to them?'

'The senior managers have already been briefed about this decision, Tom,' he said. 'And, for your information, it is a decision that affects a large number of the people present here this afternoon. A lot of managers are fond of rewarding their staff with a long lunch on Fridays, the tab for which is currently being picked up by the company. That practice has to stop, and we wanted to let everyone know that the practice is stopping not because we're ungrateful or because we're being stingy, but because we simply can't afford it anymore. Does that answer your question?'

'Not really,' said Tom.

Larry's smile did not alter. 'What more would you like to know, Tom?'

'I'd like to know how much was spent on business lunches in the past twelve months by those managers sitting behind you, and those managers sitting in the audience.'

Larry turned to Basking, who shrugged his shoulders imperceptibly.

'I'm afraid I don't have that information to hand,' said Larry.

'Have a guess,' said Tom.

'Tom, I really don't have time for this.'

'Give us a quick estimate then. Off the top of your head, tot up how many meals you and the managers have had at, say, Peacock Alley, and cost that against the number of meals eaten by managers and their staff in some cheap Italian place out in Stillorgan.'

There was a tremor in Tom's voice, which made it sound as if he was just about to break down into incoherence, but he kept it marshalled, kept it sounding clear and vigorous and purposeful.

'Okay, Tom,' said Larry, 'I hear what you're trying to say. There has possibly been a little bit too much indulgence from those of us on the podium, and that is going to stop. But it has to stop across the board.'

'So management will set the example? It'll be do as I do, not do as I say?'

'Yes,' said Larry, 'exactly. Does that address your concerns?'

'For now,' said Tom.

'We can move on then,' said Larry.

He pressed the Return key on the laptop again, and a new slide appeared: 2. OFFICE FACILITIES.

'The office,' he said. 'Now I know there have been a lot of complaints recently that the office is getting cramped, and difficult to work in. And I know that there has been talk of us moving to a larger office.'

A murmur stirred through the room; there *had* been talk of a new office, somewhere swanky down the docklands; a relocation to larger premises would make an austerity package easier to endure.

'Those rumours are not unfounded. The senior managers *have* been looking for a new office for Aisling. That's the good news. The bad news is that we can't afford to move for at least six months, maybe even a year.'

'What are we going to do in the meantime?' asked Tom.

'I was just getting to that.' He touched a button and the current slide was augmented with a new heading: 2A−HOT DESKING. 'In fact, we think we've come up with a solution that will work not only in the coming year, but when we have relocated as well.'

We think. Larry used the collective pronoun, but the expressions on the faces of the management team (with the exceptions of Dee and Aengus) conveyed very clearly that it had been all Larry's idea. Basking, in particular, looked unimpressed.

'The facts about our situation are simple: most of us don't ever have to go into the office, except during the downtime between projects. And many of the admin, support, sales and marketing staff who are notionally based in the office are frequently absent at meetings in Ireland or abroad. In other words, sometimes people who have desks are not using them and leave them idle, while people who don't have a desk occasionally need one while writing up a report on a recently completed project or researching a new one. This is not the best use of available resources, which is why I propose that we move to a "hot desk" system.'

He had until then been pacing to and fro on the podium but now he paused and swept his gaze over us. If he was waiting for someone to ask what a 'hot desk' system was, he was disappointed. He had to ask it himself, rhetorically.

'What is a hot desk system?' he asked, resuming his pacing. 'In a hot desk system, no one is assigned their own permanent desk. Instead, the office is equipped with a certain number of hot desks, where personnel can dock their laptops and make and receive phone calls.'

'That's what happens already, Larry,' said Tom.

'No, Tom, what happens at the moment is that people between projects wander around the office each day looking for an unoccupied desk, that they might then have to vacate an hour later when its "rightful" owner returns. It's very inefficient. In the new system, you'll be able to book a desk for the whole day, without worrying whether or not it is likely to be imminently reclaimed.

'Obviously, people who are always in the office—like Sheila and the PAs of the senior managers—will be assigned permanent desks. Permanent workstations will also be made available to the Tech Support team. Everyone else, though, who wants a permanent desk will have to submit to an audit to determine if the amount of time they spend in the office warrants the allocation of one.'

'It'll never work,' said Tom.

'Clearly,' said Larry, as if Tom hadn't spoken, 'it will require an adjustment in our work practices, but this is the future of work.'

'What about laptops?' asked Tom.

'What about them?'

'Does everyone get one?'

'Everyone who needs one.'

'That seems very expensive,' said Tom. 'I thought you were trying to cut costs.'

'Not everyone will get one: only those who need them.'

'In other words, only for managers.'

'It's only them … they … who will need laptops,' said Larry, momentarily tripping over which word to use. 'Most of our staff work client-site, where they are given permanent desks to work at. It's not an issue for nine-tenths of the company.'

'So what happens to these people when they're between projects?'

'We'll just have to ensure that there will always be projects for them to move onto.'

'There are gaps between projects now.'

'Then we'll manage projects better in the future. And if there are gaps, then these will be used as opportunities for training or personal development.'

'In Kilcoyle?'

'Wherever's appropriate. I don't understand why you're being so hostile, Tom.' Larry had, until that point, hardly displayed any signs of irritation at Tom's interruptions, had even seemed charmed by the contest, like a parent before an amusingly recalcitrant child, but now, for the first time, a trace of annoyance could be detected in his voice.

'You've always said that we should ask frank questions of something we don't understand. I don't understand this. It seems faddish. In a year I guarantee that we'll be back using a permanent desk system.'

'That won't happen,' said Larry. 'Not if it's managed properly.' His displeasure was now obvious.

'Larry,' said Tom, 'why should we have any confidence that it will be managed properly? You've already admitted that you mismanaged our growth this year.'

I sensed the reaction of the audience to Tom's insult but did not see it—I had my attention focused on Larry. He had until then been leaning forward, the weight of his body supported on his right leg, in the stance of a samurai poised for combat, but he now took a graceless step backwards and raised his right arm a little as if fending off an attack, as if something had been thrown at him: something physical, sharp and wounding. He turned his face away from the audience and half-glanced over his shoulder at the senior managers. I tracked all these movements, and watched as he turned back towards us and fixed his gaze on Tom, or so I assumed. That's the direction along which his line-of-sight was targeted, but I did not turn around to look. I continued to watch Larry.

'That was unfair, Tom,' he said quietly, 'very unfair. I don't know what issues you have, but I think you and I should discuss them after the meeting, in private.'

'What about your policy of openness and honesty?'

'Oh for fuck's sake, Drover, I didn't call this meeting to argue with you.'

The force of Larry's outburst silenced Tom and I glanced, I don't know why, at Dee, who was covering her mouth with her hands.

'I'm sorry, Tom,' said Larry after a elongated hush. 'I shouldn't have said that.'

'Don't be sorry,' said Tom. 'First true words spoken here this afternoon.'

'You're being very unreasonable, Tom.'

'I'm just so fucking tired of your bullshit, Larry.'

'Well you know what you can fu—,' said Larry, before he remembered himself. He smiled. 'Well at least this time you had the decency to say it to my face.'

'Absolutely,' he said, 'and I'll say this to your face as well: I quit. That should save you a bit of fucking cash.'

*

After the meeting, I felt compelled to spend the weekend as far away from Aisling as I could manage. So I bought myself a last-minute flight to London, left on Saturday morning and arrived back late on Sunday evening. It was a peculiarly liberating experience, and I bore a sense of freedom with me into the office on Monday morning, not arriving at eight as was customary for me, but at nine. As I entered, however, Sheila glanced up to see who it was, and my fine mood was ensnared immediately by her look.

She appeared worried.

More than that: fearful.

The ancient Greeks believed that malign influences could be transmitted from a person's eyes; hence the notion of the evil eye and the sign—two fingers and a thumb—by which you could reflect the influence back upon the man or woman from whom it had emanated. We do not believe such things now, of course; our ideology does not have room for 'influences'. We talk instead of moods, and about how a person's moods, especially their negative moods, can spread like a contagion through the population. We speak of the 'national mood' and the 'mood of the people' or the 'mood of the workers' with as much faith and as little reason as those who once spoke of infernal influences. So when I report to you that Sheila's anxious mood passed to me, I mean no more or less than this: I felt uneasy and I blamed this on Sheila, blamed external factors (though it was only, as any scientifically disposed individual might tell you, that her look had agitated a latent, pre-existing anxiety of which I had until then been unconscious). And more: I perceived similar signs of anxiety in every face I passed as I climbed the stairs to the third floor; perceived in every individual body a whole syntax of unexpressed tension and worry.

When I reached my desk I found a yellow post-it stuck to my monitor. *Come see me as soon as you get in*, it read, signed *D*. I looked over the partition to check that she was at her desk and saw that she was. Saw, moreover, that she was hunched over at her keyboard and in her posture there were more signs of stress, signs that only augmented my own feelings of apprehension.

'Knock, knock,' I said, when I stood beside her.

'Eoin,' she said, minimising the email she'd been working on before looking up at me. 'Have a seat.'

I pulled up a chair from the cubicle next to hers, and sat down.

'Did you have a good weekend?' she asked.

'Not bad,' I said. 'I got out of the city, to clear my head.'

'Go anywhere nice?'

'London. I managed to find a last-minute deal on the Web.'

'Lawrence tried to call you on your mobile.'

'I know, but I didn't really feel like talking to anyone from the company this weekend. Is that what this is about, Dee? Did something come up? Larry didn't leave any messages.'

'Tom's been let go.'

I blinked. 'He quit,' I said, wondering why I had to correct her on this point; she had been there after all.

'I know that,' she said, 'but we've waived the usual period of four weeks' notice. Lawrence had a chat with him on Friday night, and they agreed that it would be best if Tom left immediately.'

'Oh,' I said. I could not recall Deirdre having ever before spoken to me with such coldness or such brusqueness. I had worried that by not returning Larry's call I would make trouble for myself, and now I knew that I had: I wondered if I was about to be let go, too.

'I know you were close to him,' she went on.

'Not close, exactly,' I said.

'You were friends.'

'Not really friends either,' I said.

'You spent a lot of time with him though.'

'He's the only one I had to talk to. This floor can be a very lonely place most days.'

'Did you talk with him over the weekend?'

'I didn't talk to anyone over the weekend. Like I said, I went away to clear my head.'

'Are you sure?' She asked this question with the same cold, rehearsed formality that had so nearly caught me out at my interview. Was she trying to catch me out again?

'What's going on, Deirdre?' I asked. 'Have I done something wrong?'

She looked straight at me, but with eyes that were slightly out of focus; I got the impression that she was debating whether or not to divulge something to me: she had the look of a woman mentally rehearsing her options, calculating the consequences of choosing one over another.

'Twenty-two coders handed in their resignations this morning,' she said eventually. 'They won't admit it, but we know they've gone to form a new company with Tom.'

I stared at her. 'They did what?'

'Tom never mentioned any of this to you?'

'No,' I said. 'He never mentioned anything like this to me. We were just lunch buddies. We talked about movies and politics and rugby. Honestly. That's all.' I heard the bitterness in my own voice. For months that *is* all we had ever talked about.

'Well that's a relief,' she said, relaxing. 'I was worried that we were going to lose you too.'

'I'm here for the long haul,' I assured her.

'I'm glad to hear that. You wouldn't believe the stories I've been hearing over the weekend. Tom was talking to a lot of people in the company, trying to get them to turn against Lawrence.'

'Really?'

'Are you sure he never said anything to you along those lines?' she asked, that forensic quality once again seeping into her voice.

'Like I said, we talked about everything but work.'

'Are you sure?'

'You've asked me if I was sure twice already this morning,

Deirdre. Do you think I'm lying to you?'

'Lawrence just needs to know—I need to know—if he talked to you about this and, if he did, what he said.'

'Where is Larry?' I asked.

'He's on the phone with the clients. Damage limitation.'

'Is everyone being asked these questions?' By this I really meant, *Are you asking everyone these questions?* but it seemed more prudent to frame the question in the passive voice.

'Yes. Everyone who knew Tom well—'

'I can't imagine anyone knowing Tom well.'

'Perhaps not. But still, every manager has been asked to talk to anyone on their team who might have been on speaking terms with Tom. Which is a lot of people: he spent time on nearly every one of our client-sites in the past few months.'

'I see.'

'And you're sure there's nothing else?'

'There's nothing else. Tom never asked me to join any mutiny. And I wouldn't have gone—even if he had asked.'

'I'm glad to hear that, Eoin.' She smiled at me with her customary candidness—what I thought of as her democratic smile (because it seemed to be bestowed on everyone with equal authenticity). 'And don't take this personally.'

'Why would I take it personally, Deirdre?' I asked, responding to her smile with one of my own, though mine had less grace in it: if I was going to take anything personally it was that Tom, despite all the time we had spent together, had mentioned nothing of his plan to me.

I had, after the meeting, gone looking for him and found him standing in the hallway outside the suite, surrounded by his coterie. I stood beside him until he noticed I was there.

'That was some performance,' I said when he finally turned

to me, attempting to sound casual about it; joshing.

He gave a feral grin. 'Not how I wanted to go,' he said, 'but at least I'm gone now.'

He looked flushed, like a fighter who'd taken on an opponent two divisions above his own weight and yet somehow won, even if only on points.

'What will you do now?'

'I have a few ideas.'

Did I glance then at the people around him? They were the twenty-two who would resign en masse the following Monday. Did I suspect something?

These are the questions that occupied and obsessed me in the weeks after. And others, too, such as: Had they all been privy to some sort of plot before the meeting? Had Tom planned his disobedience, that is, or had he winged it, and persuaded the coders to his rebellion only after the fact? Had he been persuading them even as I sought him out?

But at the time I only asked, 'And you'll tell me what they are?'

'When I've figured a few things out.'

'Promise?'

'Sure.'

'And I'll see you next week.' I was aiming for an unconcerned kind of tone—*Hey, maybe I'll see you next week*, that sort of thing—because I didn't want it to sound like a question, like, *And I'll see you next week, right?* No, no, no: didn't want to make Tom think I'd miss him or anything. Didn't want to concede points to him, even then.

'Actually, I might go client-site next week,' he said. 'Keep my head out of the office until Larry and the rest of them calm down.'

'I'll see you before you leave, though, right?' This was definitely a question: I heard an unbecoming neediness in my use of the interrogative.

'My contract says I have to give at least a month's notice. I think they'll probably hold me to that, out of spite if nothing else.'

I realised that he hadn't directly answered my question, but I didn't push him. It was obvious he wanted to get back to talking to the group gathered around him.

'So I'll see you around.'

'See you around,' he said, but there was no open-endedness in his tone; there was finality. I had been dismissed.

Case Study IV

(Source: Aisling internal emails)

To: eoin.cullen@aislingltd.com
From: deirdre.heffernan@aislingltd.com
Subject: Ideas for speech
Date: 23/12/1999

eoin

Here are some ideas Lawrence asked me to type up and pass on to you. He wants you to put some shape on it for when we get back in Jan. Sorry :-(

Ideas for speech about New Economy:

A lot being spoken about the New Economy here today, and wondering whether it will live up to the hype ...

The success of the New Economy is based on the fact that it facilitates the oldest human impulse: to trade.

Ever since the first shore-dwelling Neolithic men exchanged seashells for flint axes made by their brethren living farther inland the history of trade has been the history of humanity. And, the history of humanity has been the history of trade. All the great explorations, all the great journeys, have been undertaken in the name of trade. This quest is the most consistent longing in the human heart: religions arise and then fall; wars start and then stop; political systems come and go, but trade survives it all.

The socialist and communist experiments of the twentieth century failed because they thought that the desire to trade was a by-product of capitalism, a symptom of the capitalist stage in the evolution of humanity. They could not imagine that trade is the very essence of humanity.

We have evolved to trade. In fact, if it wasn't for this impulse to trade—and all that it brings with it, including intermarriage, cultural exchange, linguistic proliferation, exploration, and so on—we, as a species, would still be wandering the African savannahs, surviving on the scavenged remains of carcasses felled by lions and leopards, competing with hyenas for the scraps.

New Economy—the entrepreneurs of the NE are like those merchant princes who were the real heroes of the Renaissance. Why? Because they challenged the Church's teaching on trade and usury, and brought wealth and riches flowing into their countries, money which was then used to patronise those men who we ordinarily think of as the great achievers of that period in history: Michelangelo, Leonardo da Vinci, etc.

The point is that all the criteria by which we measure human success since the sixteenth century could not, and would not, exist without trade. Trade is like the DNA without which the modern world could not live or grow.

The politics of greed are a distortion of the essence of trade, which is TRUST.

Still, despite trade, we are subject to repeated cycles of boom and bust economics.

New Economics, however, promises non-cyclical, linear, and exponential growth.

Why? First, because NE is not based on the production of physical commodities. The NE is based on intellectual and creative capital; its resources are not oil or minerals or metals, but ideas and patents, which are infinitely renewable (as George Bernard Shaw said about apples ... and ideas).

Second, because its channels of distribution are more integrated and less prone to disruption than was previously the case. In fact, the situation in the post-Cold War world is very similar to the situation in the late Victorian Era, when the whole world was more or less integrated into one giant market for European and American merchandise.

The present situation is MORE integrated, however. Less a trading empire and more a voluntary coalition of mutually self-interested sovereign states. Coercion replaced by cooperation; empire replaced by globalisation.

NE = intellectual capital = entertainment channels, customised medicines, software, push content, interactive computer games, knowledge repositories, e-learning libraries, personalised digital media, e-commerce.

Unlimited capital of the human mind.

End of the era of commodities. No longer will wars be fought over oil.

An era of brands, patents and ideas. What counts now are ideas, LARGE ideas.

L. wants to end with a discussion about the function of entrepreneurs in this New Economy: they are the people with the visionary ideas etc. etc.

Hopefully I'll get a chance to talk to you about these before the holidays, but if not have a great Xmas. Don't work too hard!

—Dee.

5. Mission:
Aisling's Dedication to Your Success

Once, on one of those rare afternoons when the top floor was occupied by more than just Tom and I, we turned to IM to continue a conversation we had begun during lunch.

(This was, I seem to recall, shortly after I'd joined Aisling. I record it here because it may help you understand what happened subsequently.)

Put it this way, he wrote, we talk about corporations as if they were individuals; for fuck's sake they _are_ individuals, according to the law. So does that mean they possess what we might call _consciousness_, an _individual consciousness_? Grammatically, we say 'Coca-Cola did this' or 'McDonald's did that' as easily as we say 'I did this' or 'You did that.' We don't ever say that the board of management of the Coca-Cola corporation took a decision that was passed down to the appropriate team, a decision which, upon implementation, caused the organisation to achieve more product penetration across the Horn of Africa or in Outer Mongolia or whatever the fuck it was. It's the same with us: we don't say that out of the conflicting conscious and unconscious impulses of the individual entity we know as 'John' or 'Jane' a behaviour was manifested that caused him or her to move across the room; no, we say 'John (or Jane) moved across the room,' though in fact an individual ego probably has as little actual control over the actions of its total Self as a board of management has over the actions of its total corporate body.

If that was the case, I mused, could we ever communicate with a corporation; one-on-one, I mean, just like we're communicating now?

Oh sure, he replied. We all accede to the illusion that the individual personality is a consistent, centralised unity, rather than what it really is: an uneasy and constantly shifting alliance between a diversity of drives with different goals and motivations. We could do the same for corporations. It's just a question of the _level_ of your perception. Stand back, scale it up a bit and it would require the merest of mental readjustments to find ourselves talking not to a spokesperson for Coca-Cola but to an organic part of the corporate entity, not speaking for the company but speaking _as_ the company.

Instead of talking about mergers, I wrote back, we'd talk about corporations hooking up with each other.

And a company wouldn't lay off staff, he continued, it would instead go on a corporate exercise plan, designed to help it shed its excess flab.

Christ, I typed, there'd be magazines like _Corporate Hello!_ that would report on the antics of corporations (which are shagging which; which are having affairs; which have just divorced) and be as widely read in the boardrooms of America as _Hello!_ is in the kitchens of Ireland.

Just imagine it: there'd be psychoanalysts and counsellors for companies, retained to integrate the company's various neuroses and its id impulses. Whatever the fuck it is they talk about.

LOL, I wrote back.

I'm serious, he maintained. A corporation _is_ like a person: it may shed workers and CEOs and investors may come and go, but it remains essentially the same thing, structurally, just like a person remains essentially the same, physically, even though every cell in the human body is replaced every seven years.

And what does that make workers, then? I asked.

Cells in a body.

Then teams would be like organs, I suggested, parts coming together to form a whole.

Exactly. And a company's channels of communication would pump information around the organisation like veins and arteries pump blood around the body. Like I said, just a matter of how you look at it. A higher order of perception.

I get it.

You could kill a company.

But would that make you a murderer?

From a certain point of view it would, he replied.

Actually, I wrote back, it would be more like you were a cancer, eating it away from the inside ...

*

Until Dee broke her news to the Comms Team, on a Thursday afternoon a month or so after the departure of Tom and his cohorts, I had noticed few if any disruptions in Aisling's routine, though I had been looking. Things continued as they had before, with no signs that his absence mattered, or that the events of 'The Meeting' had in any way impacted on our ability to function as a business. Deirdre's sudden, unexpected request for a meeting of the entire Comms Team was in fact the single most unusual thing that had occurred since Tom's mutiny.

It came after she had spent the morning with Larry in the boardroom. Something about the frantic energy emerging from the room had caused vague but ominous rumours to circulate the building and there was still a residue of that energy in the room as we looked at Dee in anticipation. She sat at the head of the long meeting table, and had on her face a curious expression, an expression that exhibited shards of both anxiety and nervous excitement. Yet although I sensed Dee's fretfulness, it did not disturb me in the way it was obviously disturbing Emer and Aoife (who were looking increasingly concerned); rather, a sort of lassitude settled on me. I thought I knew what it was that she would say and, besides, one of the women in the room— more than one, perhaps—was wearing a deodorant or a perfume or had washed that morning with a shower gel that smelled of stewed cherries ('Cherry Blossom', presumably, or something similar). Plus there was a citrus tang too, of the furniture polish the cleaners had used on the table the night before; the room was infused with the aromas of an old sweet shop, and I was reclining in the memories being evoked when Dee stated:

'We're being sued.'

'Shit,' said someone; someone else, not me.

'It's nothing to worry about,' she said, spreading her hands apart and holding them there, like she was demonstrating to us the length of something; I read it as a demarcating gesture—the problem is this big and no bigger. 'We'll sort it out.'

'What happened?' asked Emer. She was Aisling's graphic conceptualist, as straightforward in her speech as she was in her designs.

Before answering, Deirdre looked to make sure that the door to the room was shut. 'What I'm about to tell you goes no further than this room until I say so, OK?' she said, turning her head back to us. 'It's not general knowledge in the company yet.'

We each nodded or muttered our assent.

'Good,' she said. 'What happened is that a programmer on a systems integration project for one of the banks developed some code there for a minor routine—and no, Eoin,' she said, forestalling my question, 'I don't know what kind of routine. You know I have no idea about programming. Anyway, the problem is that he reused this routine when he was transferred to a similar project for one of the other banks.'

'I thought they weren't allowed do that,' said Emer.

'They're not,' said Dee, 'but it happens all the time. We mostly turn a blind eye to it, especially when it's just something small that the client won't notice.'

'Which bank is suing?' asked Emer. 'The one he originally worked for, or the one he was transferred to?'

'And how did they notice?' I added.

'The original bank are the ones who are suing, Emer. And, Eoin,' she said, whetting her intonation with a sceptical edge, 'we don't know yet how they found out: they haven't told us.'

'But you think it was malicious, right?'

'What makes you say that?'

'Just the way you said it,' I stammered. 'And, you know, there was that thing, *The Meeting*. Maybe there's still some resentment floating around.'

She looked at me with what I took to be a distrustful look. I felt as if she suspected I had something to do with what was going on, but then she waved her left hand from side to side and said, 'I don't think that's the case at all, but we'll find out soon enough.

'In the meantime,' she continued, slowing down her speech, and carefully emphasising each word, 'in the meantime we are going to have to get some damage limitation ready. This could hit the papers and I want to be ready if it does.'

'Are we spinning?' asked Aoife, with an enthusiasm entirely appropriate to her position as the person charged with handling the day-to-day details of Aisling's branding and PR strategies.

'Hardly,' said Dee, a little goblin's smile creasing her face, 'we're just communicating our truth.'

*

As Dee got up from the table she spotted me loitering by the door.

'You know,' she demanded, 'don't you?'

'Know what?' I asked innocently (at least, I hoped it had sounded innocent—from inside my own head it had sounded innocent), though really her question had been like a blow to my solar plexus; I felt like doubling over and getting sick.

Dee's eyes narrowed; she had that suspicious look again. I smiled.

'About Fergus,' she said.

'What about Fergus?' I asked, then answered my own question before Dee could respond, in my best you-must-be-joking tone: 'He's not the coder, is he?'

'You didn't know?'

'I had no idea.' The slant of her shoulders suggested that she believed me. She sat back down.

'Tell me about him,' she said, patting the chair beside her. I sat down. 'What's he like?'

*

I had to admit to her that I really didn't know him that well at all. He wasn't a friend, as such; I hadn't even known him before I'd moved into the spare room in his apartment down on the quays.

For the first month of my time with Aisling, I reminded Dee, I'd commuted from my parent's place, whilst searching for a place in—or close by—the city centre. Actually, I outsourced the searching to an accommodation agency that had its offices on the top storey of a building on Talbot Street. At ground level you entered a yellow door flush with the display window of a discount home-furnishings store, and then treaded up three flights of stairs into a tiny room in which four filing cabinets and two desks huddled together under a tattered and forlorn OS map of Dublin.

Liam, the partner with whom I dealt, would ring me whenever he had somewhere that he claimed matched the specifications I had listed on my application form, and give me the contact details of the letting agent for the property. The process inserted a whole new layer of mediator into finding a place to stay, but it did at least improve one's chances of arranging a viewing: if you relied on the papers alone the places in your price range were always taken before you'd even had a chance to circle them and ring the listed number.

Yet the apartments Liam recommended to me were consistently disappointing: cramped, airless, lightless basement rooms, described as 'pads'; or 'lofts' that were merely the converted attic quarters of Victorian servants. On the rare occasions on which I was shown around an apartment or a room that I liked, it was two or three hundred pounds out of my price range.

So when Fergus sent around an email to everyone in the company advertising a room in his apartment, I replied immediately, telling him that I was interested in maybe having a look.

A time was agreed.

You're looking for a big block of red-brick apartments, twenty minutes down the quays from the office, he emailed in response to my request for directions. Down past the Four Courts. The entrance is on Church Street, just around the corner from a pub called The Quill. You can't miss it.

I didn't. I left the office at seven and found the building as easily as I had been ensured I would; indeed, I was ten minutes early, so I walked up and down the quays until it was half-past and only then rang the apartment's number on the intercom. Fergus buzzed me in and came down to meet me in the courtyard.

'Eoin,' he said, offering me his hand, 'how are you?'

'Fergus,' I said, accepting and shaking, 'how's it going?'

'You don't remember me, do you?'

'Should I?'

'We were introduced at the Christmas party.'

'Were we?'

'Very briefly.'

'Sorry,' I said: 'that night's a bit of a blur.'

'For me too,' he said, laughing. 'Mostly.'

As he escorted me to the second floor I remarked to him how much it reminded me of a hotel, the long, straight, empty and thinly carpeted hallways, the cheap bright yellow paint, the blue fire doors with their little windows.

'It's easy to get turned around at first,' he agreed, 'but you get used to it.'

The door to his apartment was closed, but not locked. Beyond it there was a short, L-shaped corridor, with three more doors that I could see, all on the same side of the wall.

Fergus opened the nearest door so that I could have a peek inside. 'The bathroom,' he said, then pointed to the second door, 'That's my bedroom,' before moving past it to open the third: 'And this is the spare room.'

I looked in. The room contained one double bed (pushed up along its length on the far wall underneath a window), one white wardrobe (from Argos, I presumed) on the near wall, and a narrow space between the two.

'It's a bit tight,' he said.

'All I need is someplace to lay my head,' I replied. 'Has anyone else been around to see it yet?'

'No one else has even gotten in touch with me, so it's all yours—if you want it.'

He had already told me by email the rent he was looking for; it was fifty pounds more than I'd budgeted for, but the room was by far the best I'd seen and I was tired of the quest and I realised that I might not find a better deal so I said, 'I'll take it,' and we shook hands again.

'It's a deal,' he said.

We went into the sitting-room-cum-kitchen (located behind a door just beyond the turn in the hallway) and over tea agreed that I would move my stuff in that coming weekend. My father brought it all in a few carloads on Saturday afternoon and then Fergus and I went for a pint, had a good laugh, didn't talk about work at all, and I thought with relief that at least my flatmate isn't a gobshite but after that I hardly saw him. He worked as a team leader for a client based in Stillorgan, and spent most weekday nights (most weekends, too) at his girl-friend's place in Dun Laoghaire. The only reason, he told me once, that he didn't rent out his room as well, and officially move in with her, was that they sometimes had huge fuck-off rows and he felt that he still needed a place where he could crash and cool-off.

I mentioned most—but not all—of this to Dee, and I also mentioned most-but-not-all of what happened on the Friday after Tom had quit the company, when I thought I heard a key fumbling in the lock of the apartment door a little after one in the morning. I had gone to bed around eleven but hadn't been able to sleep so I was sitting up at the time, trying to numb my eyes into submission with MTV. I turned down the volume and yes, there was definitely someone scraping a key over the lock without, however, managing to insert it successfully.

I was already on my way to the door when whoever it was—Fergus, or someone from another flat maybe, struggling at the wrong door in their inebriation—began to knock at the door: 'Eoin,' they whisper-shouted between raps, 'Eoin, are you in there?'

I opened the door to find that it was Fergus, plastered; I could smell the drink on his breath, and he stood askew, his hands grasping either jamb in order to preserve his upright position.

'Laoise threw me out,' he said. 'I got stroppy.'

He didn't make any move to enter and I suspected that he

was waiting for me to invite him in, which I did, standing aside to give him some berth.

'Not interrupting anything, am I?' he asked with exaggerated courtesy, meaning, I suppose, had I a girl in the flat.

'You're not interrupting anything,' I assured him, following as he staggered into the living room. 'Not tonight.'

'Fucking hell,' he said, flopping into one of the armchairs with a sound halfway between a sigh and a spit.

'Do you want a cup of tea?' I asked.

'Tea'd be lovely,' he said. 'And something to eat. Do we have anything in to eat?'

'I could make you some toast.'

'No,' he said, considering this, 'I need something a bit stronger than toast, something *greasy*.'

'Fried eggs?'

'Fried eggs would be fucking mighty,' he proclaimed.

I went into the kitchen alcove, hoping that he wouldn't fall asleep while I was in there, but when I brought out his tea and the eggs and toast I had made him, he was alert in the armchair, flicking through the channels with the remote.

'Lovely,' he said, taking the mug and the plate. 'You not having anything?'

'I had a big dinner.'

'You shouldn't have gone to any trouble, not for me.'

'It was no trouble.'

'Well,' he said, saluting me with the sandwich he had made, 'lucky the woman that gets ye.'

'So Laoise threw you out,' I said.

'She wouldn't even let me in,' he said, 'the bitch. I'm fucking finished with her this time.'

'You don't mean that.'

'I fucking do,' he said fiercely. 'I mean I know we'd planned to go out and everything but I explained to her that the boys on the team were a bit upset and needed to go out for a few scoops.'

'Why were they upset?' I asked.

'Jesus,' he said, 'you know. You were there.'

'The Tom thing?'

'Of course the Tom thing,' he said belligerently. He swallowed the last of his sandwich and hiccupped. 'Tom was a smart fucking cunt.'

'That he was,' I agreed.

'And he didn't go along with all that hippie crystal shite Larry's always trying to foist on us.'

'He was much too smart to fall for that.'

'Exactly,' said Fergus with spirit, pointing his left index finger at me. 'Much too smart—exactly.'

'And your team? What do they think about Larry now?'

'They think he's lost the plot completely.' He slid down into the chair, and pulled the coat he had not yet taken off snugly around him. 'They think that you just can't take that shite seriously or it would send you fucking cracked.

'I joined Aisling to program,' he went on. 'I didn't join to be brainwashed.'

'I know what you mean,' I said.

'No you don't,' he protested. 'No you fucking don't. You're always fucking defending him.'

'Not anymore.' I adopted a pacifying tone. I was worried that his aggression would, if stoked up too much, prove difficult to quench and that I'd have a fight on my hands, or a shouting match, that we'd wake the neighbours, have the Guards calling round asking, *Now, gentlemen, what's the trouble here?*

'What changed your mind? Tom, right?'

'Of course,' I agreed, choosing my words carefully. 'If Larry was as open-minded as he says he is, Tom would still be working for Aisling.'

'Too fucking right he would. He's always going on about inclusive this, open-minded that, blah blah big bleeding blah, but he can't stand anyone questioning what he preaches. And in my book that's a cult, a fucking cult.'

'I didn't know you felt so strongly about it.'

'Maybe it took what happened to Tom to bring it into ... to bring it into ...' He struggled to find the right word to finish the sentence and twirled his left index finger, as if the word he sought was at the end of an invisible thread that would come within his reach if he could but wind it up.

But he didn't seem to be getting any closer. 'Bring it into focus?' I suggested.

'Focus!' he said, stilling his finger's motion. 'Focus,' he repeated.

'If you feel so strongly you should say something.'

'And where do you think that would get me? It would get me fired, that's what it would get me. Fucking fired.'

'If you hate Larry so much, I don't understand why that's a problem.'

He looked across at me, and I at him, the first time in the conversation that we had looked directly at each other, our eyes having previously been trained on the muted pictures on the television-screen. He looked angry, as if I had insulted him, but when he spoke, he spoke softly: 'I have a mortgage,' he said simply. 'I can't afford not to have a job.'

'There are plenty of jobs out there. We're the fastest growing economy in Europe. It's an employees' market.'

'I guess so.'

'It would let Larry know that not everyone is enamoured of his vision.'

Fergus considered this for a moment before asking, sharply, 'Why can't you fucking say something?'

'Everyone would think I'd done it because I was friends with Tom. It wouldn't mean as much coming from me.'

There was another silence in which we both turned to look again at the television. He eventually said, shrugging his shoulders, 'I'll think about it.'

*

Dee sat looking at her hands, which she had placed palm-up in her lap during my selective retelling of the story.

'I see,' she said when I'd finished. She looked up and smiled as if I'd been telling her some fitfully entertaining anecdote. 'Well.'

'Well,' I said, returning her smile.

'Thanks,' she said.

'It doesn't mean anything,' I insisted. 'He was drunk. I'm sure this is just a mistake or a coincidence or something.'

'You're probably right.'

'I wouldn't have said anything if I thought you would hold it against him.'

'I appreciate your loyalty,' she said. The peculiar emphasis she invested in the word *loyalty* confused me; I couldn't tell if she was touched by my protectiveness towards Fergus, or if she was insinuating that such faithfulness was equivalent to a lack of fidelity towards her and Larry, and had been noted.

'What are you going to do?' I asked.

'I'm going to think. You can leave now, Eoin,' she said in a voice laced with disappointment. And I did: I left. I smiled weakly at her as I went, wondering if her disappointment was with me, straitened by the thought that it probably was, but also feeling relieved of a burden that had been lately weighing down on me; feeling, well, *reprieved*.

*

I expected that I wouldn't hear any further news about Fergus's indiscretion for a while, that it might even be resolved without the whole company finding out, but the bank escalated the matter and insisted that they'd pursue Aisling to the courts if Larry wasn't seen to deal firmly with the problem.

Thus I wasn't surprised, when I returned home to the apartment three days after Dee had broken the news to the Comms Team, to find the locks undone and Fergus slumped in his armchair, cycling through the channels with the remote.

When I entered the room he turned his head to look at me and asked me, 'Did you hear what they fucking did?'

I shrugged my shoulders to indicate that *yes, I had heard*.

'They've fucking suspended me,' he went on, as if he hadn't seen my reaction, or had misinterpreted it, thought I'd been telling him that I'd heard nothing.

My inclination was to tell him that it wasn't nearly as bad as it could have been—they could have just fired him—but it probably wasn't what he wanted to hear, so what I actually said was, 'I don't think they can do that. Can they?'

'Apparently. They say it's in my contract.'

He rattled the sheaf of paper that lay on his stomach, which was parallel to the cushion on which he was half-sitting, half-lying; his buttocks hung over the lip of the chair.

I took my usual place on the sofa. 'How are you doing?' I asked, flinching at my use of such a banal platitude, but feeling that something needed to be said, anything.

'Been better,' he said, spiking the words with sarcasm, then added, 'I'm going to lose my job, amn't I?'

'You did nothing that hasn't been done by loads of other people in the company. Everyone reuses code.'

'But not everyone blabs about it.'

'Is that what happened?' I asked the question in an offhand way, even though I desperately wanted to hear what he believed had really happened; what suspicions, if any, he had.

'I don't know. I suppose so. I can't think of any other explanation. I must have skulled one too many pints at a client do, and let it slip.'

'Well there you go then,' I said, 'it wasn't your fault.'

'Oh fuck yeah, that's going to work as a defence: sorry the company's in trouble, Larry, but I got steamed at a party. Hope you understand.'

I couldn't say anything to that. I leaned back on the sofa.

'What am I going to do?' he asked, his voice pitched up to near panic.

'I think you should be honest,' I said, leaning forward again. 'Be honest and tell Larry exactly what happened.'

'Can I ask a favour, man?'

'Of course,' I said, though I dreaded the request.

'Talk to Larry for me, would you?'

'I don't know—'

'Oh come on, Eoin, you're in the inner circle. You and Larry are friends, for fuck's sake.'

'I wouldn't say friends, exactly ...'

'You're fucking closer to him than I am.'

'I guess.'

'And you have a better chance of making him see that this was all just a big mistake.'

I was reluctant to give him a positive answer, because I didn't want Larry and Dee to have any further doubts about my loyalty, but still, it might work to my advantage: a display of loyalty— even if directed at the wrong source—might be better than a display of no loyalty at all.

'I'll see what I can do—'

'Great.'

'—but don't get your hopes up. I can't promise anything.'

'And don't mention I was drunk. Just tell him I was tipsy.'

'Sure.'

'Thanks, man. I really appreciate this. I know I bitch about Larry but I really like my job, I do, and I don't want to be fired. At the very least, ask him if he's going to blackball me with other employers.'

'I will.'

'I owe you a pint.'

'Listen, if I can pull this off you'll owe me the whole fucking brewery.'

'Absolutely: the whole fucking brewery. You'll never have to buy a pint of Guinness again.'

'I'll hold you to that.'

'Sure you will. I'd hold me to that if I was in your place.'

*

It took me a week to secure some time with Larry. Every evening Fergus asked me if I'd managed to have a word with the Big

Man, and I was tempted, more than once, to lie and say that I had and it had changed nothing, but I only shrugged and said, 'Not yet, maybe tomorrow.'

When Larry and I did talk it wasn't in the office. A cubicle had been cleared for Larry on the second floor, but he never used it except as a place to store the books and magazines he eventually meant to get around to reading. If he needed to work in the office he took over the boardroom for himself; if he wanted to have a word with you in private he brought you to Café Trieste, just around the corner. And it was there he suggested we go when I found him in the boardroom early one morning and told him that I had something to say to him.

'What are you having?' he asked, when the waitress came to take our order.

'A latte,' I said, 'decaf.'

'Decaf?'

'I've been drinking far too much caffeine lately,' I explained. 'I need to detox.'

He nodded. 'I'll just have a green tea,' he said. When she'd gone, he leaned forward over the table, closing the gap between us. 'What's this about?'

I leaned forward too. 'It's about Fergus, Fergus Ree.'

'Go on,' he said, keeping his voice admirably stable but unable, nonetheless, to suppress an involuntary tensing of the muscles of his neck and shoulders.

'I just want to preface what I'm about to say with the caveat that I'm speaking for Fergus because no one else seems to be on his side, not because I agree with what he did.'

'Sure,' said Larry, but he sounded unconvinced.

'Fergus feels that what happened wasn't his fault. Everyone reuses code. He feels he's being scapegoated.' I modulated my delivery to convey the impression that I was doing this only out of sympathy for Fergus, not because I believed the story he'd asked me to tell.

Larry blinked. 'I see,' he said.

'You don't agree?'

'It's not that I don't agree. But reusing code is not the issue. The issue is that the client found out.'

'Right.'

'And that's unforgivable.'

'Fergus claims he never talked to the client—at least, not deliberately.'

'What does that mean?' asked Larry.

'It means that he might have let it slip at a client party, after he'd had a little too much to drink.' I know Fergus had asked me not to say this, but I felt like I had no choice: Larry needed an explanation, as he'd think Fergus had acted with premeditation.

But the explanation didn't please him. His eyes narrowed, and a vicious expression surfaced, then as quickly subsided, on his face. He remained mute while he tried to control his reaction. 'Well,' he said at last, 'that's OK then.'

'Jesus, Larry, I'm sorry. I didn't mean to upset you.'

'And I'm sorry for snapping, Eoin, but one drunken conversation between Fergus and a client might well destroy my business and I'm not going to let that happen.'

'Of course not,' I agreed.

'And I think we both know that even if this whole thing was an accident, Fergus harboured some resentment towards the company. Wouldn't you say?'

I nodded.

'Well then,' he said, glancing away.

Silence. I sipped my latte.

'What do you want me to do?' he asked eventually, his gaze remaining averted.

'I don't know. Whatever you have to. Fergus just asked me to put in a word for him. Let you know that he didn't do it on purpose.'

'Fine,' he said, but it was *fine* used in its dismissive sense.

'How bad does it look?'

'Bad,' he said, allowing his line-of-sight to drift back into contact with mine. 'If no one comes forward with any alternative testimony then he's gone—he'll be let go.'

'That's it?'

'That's it: unless he can prove that he wasn't the one who talked to the client.'

'And what happens then? Will Fergus get a reference, or is he going to be blackballed?' Larry looked quizzically at me. 'You know,' I explained, 'are you going to do a "he'll-never-work-in-this-town-again" number on him?'

'He's not going to be blackballed, and he'll get a good reference from us, because he's a decent programmer. But,' he added, holding up the index finger of his right hand in an authoritative gesture, 'I'll make sure that anyone who asks about him will be told that they probably shouldn't trust him with confidential information.'

As Larry talked I swirled some coffee around the rim of my cup, collecting the clumps of foam that clung to the inner plane.

'I know that seems a bit harsh,' he said, as if sensing that I still needing persuading, 'but we all have to speak our truths, and this is my truth about Fergus. I wouldn't feel right if I didn't tell another company exactly how Fergus had performed with us.'

I drained my cup. 'I understand,' I said, with an ingratiating smile.

'Good. Are we done here?'

'We're done,' I said.

*

No one came forward to offer any testimony that would exonerate Fergus so, shortly after my conversation with Larry, he was let go. He wasn't, however, as inconvenienced by the decision as he had feared he would be: he joined an agency, and they quickly found work for him, work he enjoyed doing—work that earned him nearly as much as he'd been earning with Aisling.

'Best fecking thing that ever happened to me,' he said, 'getting kicked out of that place.' This was maybe a month afterwards. I was still renting the room in his apartment. 'I don't know how you can stick it.'

'Oh I'm looking,' I lied, adding, 'the atmosphere has really soured.'

This latter statement was not a lie: the mood in the company *had* gone bad, though I experienced it as an intangible shift in tone, rather than as any quantifiable change in activity. In fact, there were few discernable changes made as a result of Fergus's sacking, at least in the daily running of the company. Every team leader was given a talking to, and a policy document reiterating the principles of client confidentiality was circulated to everyone who had access to sensitive information. But, aside from this, things went on as they had before: people performed the tasks they had performed before; projects were managed, sales contracts pursued, information distributed, wages calculated, invoices issued, et cetera, et cetera. Just like always.

It was a good façade.

But you can usually tell when someone is in a depression,

even if they smile and tell you that everything is fine: something about their energy, or lack thereof, alerts you to what they won't themselves admit. Similarly, someone familiar with the company, but not of the company, a regular visitor to our offices—a sales rep, say, or a business partner—would have picked up on the change, though they probably wouldn't have been able to say exactly what it was they'd tuned into. They would have left the building and later remarked to their boss, or to a colleague, on how the ambience in Aisling had changed, *Can't put my finger on it exactly, but something is definitely different.*

I'm not sure we could have articulated the changes ourselves; the corporate self in denial and all that. It was anyway an elusive transformation; and if you were aware of it at all, you felt it as a kind of collective sullenness. It was like knowing, without having to think about it, that both you *and* the person you were talking to were in a bad mood and, intuiting, what's more, that your mood and theirs was essentially the same mood and that this mood was, in turn, part of a larger, collective mood: that the mood was not so much in you as you were in it.

And it wasn't only psychological, this sensation of being a constituent part of something, something larger than myself (no, not even a part, nothing so mechanical—more like being an ephemera, a thought conceived in a mind vaster than one's own); it had a physical effect too—people in the office began to look tired and stressed and edgy. Dee, in particular, seemed increasingly drained, her sallow skin gone mushroom-white, her eyes a bit sunken, rimmed with dark pouches, and her long, dark, dyed hair less lustrous than before.

I told myself that it had nothing to do specifically with the departures of Tom and Fergus; it was no more mysterious than a sports team going through the equivalent of a losing streak and not inevitably indicative of a company on its way to the glue factory. Things would return to normal when things began going right for the company again.

But things didn't begin to go right. There were rumours that the Board was putting pressure on Larry to give Basking more of a role in the company's strategic operations, and certainly there were lots of reports of conference rooms in city-centre hotels being booked for intense, high-level summits that lasted from Friday evening to Sunday afternoon.

People used to come to us, the Comms Team, for information, *Do you know what the fuck is going on?*, but even though we were at the frontline of trying to put things right—arranging interviews, placing ghost-written articles, issuing press releases— we were only provided with as much information as we needed and hardly knew more than the rest of the staff.

But we all knew this: New sales became harder to make. Also: Long-standing clients became more demanding and less willing to be talked into extending or renewing existing contracts. And: Articles began to appear in the print and online business media detailing Aisling's real or imagined ills.

And yet, despite everything, I would have to concede that things did seem to have reached a kind of equilibrium, were coming under control again, when the whole b2gb.com thing broke.

*

The founder of www.bout-to-go-bust.com (or www.b2gb.com for short) was Robert Pound, my former boss at *Wake.com*, who had wild-goosed it to San José after the collapse of the magazine to join a tech start-up out there.

I knew this because soon after joining Aisling I signed up to the Irish Internet Advocacy mailing list and discovered that not only had Bob been a founding member, but that he also still occasionally posted to the list, keeping its members appraised of his quest for success in Silicon Valley. There was, however, as 1999 drew to a close, a sense of increasing desperation in his *communiqués*. Whereas before he would, every couple of weeks, have distributed an email telling us how close his company was to going IPO and what he planned to do with his share of the swag, now he sent missives full of accounts of secret management meetings and rumours of imminent bankruptcy.

And, indeed, in early 2000 his company did go Chapter 11 and laid off most of its development staff, including Bob. After three years, he was left with no return on his considerable investment of time except an extensive portfolio of rancour—and the wit to use it.

Dear friends, he wrote in an email he sent to the list on the day he was laid off, my company has been in trouble for some time. Well, the truth is, as I found out today, they were in BIG trouble, and filed for bankruptcy this morning. Worse, they fired us—also this morning.

I am using this server remotely (and illegally!) to send messages to everyone who contacts me at this work address to let you know what happened (I didn't get a chance this morning, seeing as we were all escorted out of the building by security as soon as we were told the bad news!!!).

Anyway, I expect this pipe will be cut off at any moment (they fired all the tech guys, too, but they'll twig soon) so I'll keep this short.

I want to first of all assure you that all is not lost with me because I've had a contingency plan in place for a while (the writing was on the wall here weeks ago), so drum-roll, please: Ladies and gentlemen, I have set up my own e-commerce website.

I realise that this might seem a bit foolish in the current economic climate, but I think I have a business plan that can't possibly fail—because it's focused on failure!

My website is called 'bout-to-go-bust.com' (b2gb.com). I've just uploaded it, so check it out and let me know what you think. And feel free to post your comments—after all, this is a website for pissed-off employees and ex-employees of IT companies everywhere in the world, not just here in Silicon Valley.

Cheers!—Bob.

P.S.—Don't forget to buy a T-shirt.

This last comment referred to the fact that he intended to make his money selling T-shirts, mouse-pads and mugs engraved with the b2gb logo and branded with slogans such as 'My company went bust and all I got was this lousy T-shirt (which I had to buy myself)' printed on them.

I'm not sure if the site ever became a serious money-making venture, and it's closed down now, but it fulfilled its original purpose—to provide a forum where irate cubicle serfs could vent their spleen—commendably. It became infamous, actually, in its own way. Industry journalists began using it as an indicator of the state of health of the major players in the New Economy. The news about boohoo.com's imminent closure was, for instance, first broken on b2gb by one of boohoo's employees, a fact that prompted *Wired* to do a big profile on Robert and the site.

More importantly, staff in Internet companies in the US, Canada, the UK, Ireland, Australia, New Zealand and elsewhere, checked in on the site regularly—to see if anyone was talking about *their* company. No mentions and you were probably in the clear. A couple of mentions and it might be time to start circulating your CV. If your company was, however, in the Red Zone (twelve mentions or more), the best thing to do was clean your desk, delete anything incriminating from your hard drive, and prepare for the inevitable.

Aisling awoke one morning to find itself well into b2gb's Red Zone. Worse, there was also a report about it in the business pages of *The Irish Times*, which added to the seriousness of the problem. I hadn't, however, read the paper when I got into work, so when I was stopped on the way to my desk by Emer, who asked if I'd heard, I replied, 'Heard what?'

She told me about the story in the *Times*. 'You don't seem surprised,' she said, when she'd finished. 'Do you know something we don't?'

'Of course not,' I said. 'It's just that I thought you were going to tell me the company had gone bust or something like that.'

'That could still happen,' she said. 'They're all in the boardroom, all the bigwigs—Larry, Basking, Dee, that eejit from Essentia, the whole lot. I wouldn't be surprised if bad news didn't come strutting out of there with them.'

'You think?'

'I have a feeling,' she said, with a fatalistic toss of her head.

An hour later, Dee called from her mobile and asked me to meet her in the Trieste.

'Was that Dee?' asked Emer when I passed her cubicle on my way to the stairs. 'What did she say?'

'Just that she needed to talk. In the café around the corner.'

'She's never done that before, has she?'

'Done what?'

'Asked someone to meet her outside the office.'

'Not that I know of.'

'Must be serious.'

'It's probably nothing.'

Emer arched her brows and said, 'Best of luck anyway.'

I nodded my appreciation, though I couldn't tell if the gravity of her tone was mockery or an attempt at genuine sympathy.

'Cheers,' I said.

*

I found a cappuccino waiting for me when I joined Dee in the café.

'Is that for me?' I asked after I'd sat down.

She nodded.

'Thanks.'

'I hope you don't mind meeting here,' she said, 'but I needed a fag.'

'I didn't know you smoked,' I said.

'I quit after college.' She held up the smouldering tip of her cigarette. 'I've started again. You want one?'

'I have my narcotic right here,' I said, tipping my cup towards her. 'Thanks.'

She nodded again and pursed her lips together in imitation of a smile—*You're welcome*—but didn't say anything. I waited for her to speak, but she remained silent, staring down at her cup.

'What's this about, Dee?' I asked after an uncomfortable interlude.

'You've heard what's going on?'

It was my turn to nod mutely. The oddly flat way in which she was modulating her voice and her refusal to sustain eye contact caused my fear (which had until then only existed as a potential) to jump the gap from inert to live. I knew that I was going to be fired, that she suspected I'd been involved in every-thing that had happened—and was happening—to the com-pany. Sweat twitched through the pores on my chest and fore-head and in my armpits, and my right arm and left leg both began to judder. I wanted to get up and walk out the door, but couldn't, not without appearing guilty: trapped.

'Am I being let go?' I asked, though what I had intended to voice with a strong and demanding cadence was choked by a contraction of my vocal cords and came out as a dry whisper.

'What?' She flicked her attention back from whatever other place it had been. She smiled—really smiled, one of her radi-antly egalitarian smiles—and said, 'No, nothing like that.' She took a sip of her coffee. 'I'm sorry if I seem odd, but it's been a strange morning.'

'What's going on exactly? No one in the office knows, not really. It's all rumours and speculation.'

'Lawrence and Padraig are fielding calls from our creditors and clients, trying to sort this thing out. Have you ever heard of this bloody website? I didn't know it existed until I opened the paper this morning.'

'I've heard of it,' I said. 'There was a piece about it in *Wired* last month.' I paused, then asked, 'Is it true, though? Are we in financial trouble?'

'No,' she snapped. 'It's a lie. Someone spreading malicious rumours.'

Someone. 'Do you have any idea who did it?' I asked in another croak. 'Do you think it was an employee of Aisling?'

'We're not sure,' she said. 'We don't have any evidence. But I'd bet it was Tom or one of his cronies.' She aspirated the name so that it sounded as if she had spat it out, not spoken it: *Tom-hh*.

'You think Tom did this?' It was a struggle to keep the relief out of my voice.

'I wouldn't put it past him.'

I considered my next statement carefully, wondering what it might cost me, but deciding it was worth the risk: 'It doesn't seem like Tom's style.'

'It seems exactly like his style,' she said passionately. 'Don't go trying to defend him.'

'I'm not trying to defend him, I'm just saying it seems a little vindictive, that's all. Whatever his grievances, Tom always struck me as more fair-minded that that.'

'It could be one of the other defectors,' she conceded.

I laughed, lightly, at her choice of words. 'You make it sound like we're involved in some kind of cold war.'

'It seems more and more like we are,' she said seriously. 'He's made it clear that he has no qualms about poaching clients from us, and after that stunt with the code ...'

'But Tom had nothing to do with that,' I protested, but my suspicions were aroused. She looked guilty, as if she had said more than she should; but this expression passed, replaced by an expression of resolve.

'We found out how the bank knew about Fergus's reuse of code,' she stated, as if the information would be news to me.

'I know,' I said slowly: 'Fergus admitted that he'd let it slip when he was drunk.'

'Someone sent them an email.'

'Who sent who an email?' I asked, confused by her imprecise use of pronouns.

'Someone sent the bank an email.'

'Why would Fergus do that?' I asked, knowing that I sounded

a bit thick, but her obliqueness was confusing me, and I needed clarification.

'Not Fergus,' she said. 'It was someone else. Someone other than Fergus sent the bank an email detailing exactly how and where Fergus had reused his code.'

From her expression and posture, I realised that she thought I would find this information shocking. 'Do you know who it was?' I asked in another slow, hoarse whisper, before adding, with a flash of clarity, 'How do you know it wasn't Fergus? I mean, he might have made up that story about being drunk to cover his tracks.'

'I'm not saying he wasn't involved, but we don't think he sent the actual email.'

I considered this statement for several seconds. 'You don't think he sent the actual email,' I said, repeating her words as a means of illuminating my own understanding.

'No.'

'Which means that you don't know who did send it.'

'It came from an anonymous email address,' she admitted: '2fingers2aisling@hotmail.com.'

'Then Fergus might not be involved at all,' I exclaimed, though I didn't like how I sounded; a bit too Perry Mason, a bit too theatrical. 'He might be innocent.'

'He might,' she said, without sounding convinced.

'How long have you known this?' I asked, curious, but also accusatory.

'Not long,' she said, defensively. 'Lawrence had to fight to get the information out of the bank. He always thought there was more going on than just a drunken lapse at a party.'

'Then why did he fire Fergus?' More accusatory than curious now.

'He knew that the bank wanted to see how he'd react.'

'That's a bit bloody Irish,' I said. 'Why didn't they just tell him the truth?'

She shook her head. 'Maybe they thought we were trying to put one over on them.'

'Jesus, Dee,' I said, 'this is very fucking complicated.' She smiled in what I took for a self-pitying manner: *Welcome to my world.*

'And you still have no idea who sent the email?' She shook her head again. 'Can't you trace it?'

'We did trace it,' she said, 'to a cyber café in London.'

'I see,' I said, wondering if she knew more than she was letting on. 'That's something to go on.'

'It's nothing to go on,' she snapped. 'The person using the computer paid cash, and the owners of the café don't keep records, or have security cameras.'

My instinct was to say nothing, but I had to ask, 'Have you called the Guards?'

'We have. They can't do anything. They say that no crime has been committed; as far as they're concerned it's a civilian matter. Plus, it's in another jurisdiction and I don't think they extradite people for sending malicious emails.' She leaned forward to stub out her fag. 'We're thinking of hiring a private detective.'

'Do they have those in Ireland?' I asked, as blasé as I could manage.

'I know,' she said, smiling without warmth, 'it sounds totally Hollywood, doesn't it?'

I smiled in return. 'Is there anything I can do?' I adopted a positive tone of voice, wanting to reassure her that I was part of the team. Ready to muck in, do what's necessary.

She thought about this for a moment. 'Actually there is,' she said. 'It's why I called you here to talk, in fact.' She hesitated. 'You may not like it.'

I waited for her to continue. My heart, which had calmed itself down since the start of the conversation, began to rapidly batter itself against my clavicle again, and my skin tightened, exposing the sweat lying underneath, like the residue revealed when salt pans dry and crack in the heat of the sun.

'I know you and Tom were friends—'

'Jesus, Dee, how many times—?'

'No, listen,' she said, 'we want to use that.'

Ah.

'Lawrence has heard that Tom is bidding for a project that some crowd called Ninth Wave have put out to tender,' she explained. 'He wants us to submit a counter-bid.'

'What does he want me to do?'

'He wants you to help him get inside Tom's head. He wants you to help him figure out what kind of offer Tom would make, and how he might write it, so that we can write an offer of our own, a better offer.'

'Of course,' I said, 'anything.' My stomach unclenched. My skin slackened. My heart began to slow its desperate sprint. 'Anything at all, Dee, you know that.'

*

As we walked out of the Trieste I thought back to the time, not so long ago now, when Dee had dismissed me from the board-room after I'd told her what I knew about Fergus. I remembered how I had felt at being sent away by her: not angry, as I might have been angry with someone else (with Larry, for instance, or Tom); or, rather, yes, angry, but angry mostly with myself for having caused Dee to act in such a manner.

I felt something similar now, only more so, more acute. As we exited onto the street, she set her shoulders against a squall of wind barging its way up from the river. She seemed lost. Weary. I felt a huge, silly, chivalrous urge to put my arm around her and tell her that everything would be OK and my right arm did reach out towards her, but only to touch her elbow.

How are you doing? I wanted to ask, but that somehow got turned aside. What actually came out was a question asking how Larry was holding up.

'I haven't really talked to him about it,' she said. 'We've both been busy, you know.' She smiled wistfully, and her eyes moistened, although that could have been the effect of talking into the bitter breeze.

'I'm sure he's dealing with it just fine,' she added. 'Let's get back to the office.'

'Sure,' I said, walking in step beside her. I wanted more than anything to reach out and take her hand, to comfort her, to hold her, to more than hold her, but I snorted inwardly and told myself not to be ridiculous, she wouldn't be interested, and anyway, what would Larry say? What about his prohibition?

Yes, yes, totally out of the question, and she had a boyfriend, whom I had met, but I now understood that what was happening was harming the company, really harming it. And although I didn't care if Basking got hurt, or Aengus, or even Larry, I cared about Dee getting hurt. Cared about her? Was that it? Yes, that was it: cared about her. And I suddenly understood that I cared *for* her, too, in whatever way you want to understand that phrase, and that by staying at Aisling to prove a point to Larry (and to prove a point to Tom as well) I had cost Dee something, and cost myself something too.

I would make amends. I would repay her for her troubles. And although yes of course it made me uneasy to think that my idealism and faith had once again come down to this—to a woman—I persuaded myself that what had happened with Erin would not happen with me and Deirdre, simply because there was no prospect of us ever being intimate. None whatsoever.

Case Study V

(Source: Aisling internal emails)

To: team.leaders@aislingltd.com
From: comms.team@aislingltd.com
Subject: Updated confidentiality guidelines
Date: 22/06/2000

Dear everyone,
I am sure you are all aware of the difficulties we experienced recently arising out of a breach of client confidentiality.

This is not a trivial issue. It goes to the heart of what we do. If our clients can't trust us, then there is no point in our continuing to do business.

The number one rule of consulting is, has been, and always will be: keep your client's secrets. This is especially true when your clients include one or more companies who are in direct competition with each other in information-sensitive sectors such as banking or the financial services.

The notion of confidentiality extends to, and includes, not deliberately reusing algorithms across projects for clients in competition with each other.

We understand that this can seem like an impossible ask, but clients demand a certain level of operational amnesia on our behalf. It is one of the challenges of operating as a consultancy. Clients want to be assured that not only will you refrain from even hinting to a competitor the exact nature of the project you are working on for them, but they also want to be constantly assured that you are not applying expertise you may have gained working for them on a problem being experienced by a competitor.

During Aisling's induction course, it is impressed upon every new member of staff that they are to discuss their work with members of their team only, and then only as necessary. Furthermore, that they are to avoid discussing their work with Aisling staff members working on other projects. Finally, that they are to make sure that they unlearn what they might have previously learned if they are transferred to a project for a company in competition with their former client.

We would like all team leaders to convene a meeting of their teams within the week, and reiterate these fundamental points. If anyone raises any objections (we understand that this can seem like an inefficient way of doing business and, to a programmer, even counter-intuitive) then please reiterate that it must be understood that these measures are the price of working for a consultancy.

If they continue to object please explain to them that we are not holding them against their will, and they are free to redirect their career outside the company.

Questions should be directed to Deirdre Heffernan at extn 1132.

Sincerely,

The Comms Team

6. Values:
The Aisling Commitment to Integrity

The Friday after we were informed that we'd secured the Ninth Wave deal (beating out bids from a number of the other big consultancies, as well as a bid from Tom's company) Larry treated the Project Team to dinner, though we were to understand, he explained more than once, that he was paying for it himself. It was his treat. He was in no way contravening the company's austerity guidelines.

Which I suppose is the reason he took us to a cheap and not particularly distinguished Italian place in Temple Bar. But I didn't pay attention to the food. Rather, I contrived to find myself sitting opposite Dee, and paid all my attention to her, though she hardly paid any to me, talking and laughing with the person seated beside her. Once or twice, however, she turned to me and smiled, which caused my blood to flush with whatever biochemical it is that regulates hope. Oh I had no illusions. It was enough just to be in her presence, to sit across from her, feeling touched, if only peripherally, by what Larry would have called her energy, although (OK, I admit it) I couldn't help contemplating what it would be like to be enveloped entirely in that field, to be enveloped entirely in her.

We loitered at our tables until eight o'clock, when the waiting staff asked us if we wouldn't mind kindly vacating so that they could accommodate the second sitting of the evening. After everyone had eventually gathered on the street in front of the restaurant Larry suggested going for a few pints, but it had been a long week and most of us had to get up early the next morning to catch the minibus down to Castletownbere. Larry looked disappointed as the group drifted apart; he didn't drink himself, not much, but until a few months ago there would have been no question of the lot of us going on the razz, regardless of how early we had to get up the next day, and I'm sure he felt that a night on the batter would have been an indication that things were OK with Aisling again.

Finally just myself and Larry and Dee remained.

'Well,' he said, slapping his hands together, 'I guess I should get going too. Early start and all that.' He smiled with a bit of a stupid grin.

Neither Dee nor I replied.

'It's a pity you're not coming with us to Cork, Deirdre,' he went on.

'I wasn't invited,' she said.

'Weren't you?'

'No,' she said, then, condescendingly, 'I wouldn't have gone anyway, you know I'm not into that Boys' Own stuff.'

'No, of course not,' he said. 'See you on Tuesday, then.'

'Goodbye, Lawrence,' she said.

'Eoin, I'll see you tomorrow. Nice and early.'

'Nice and early,' I said and watched as he turned and walked up Crown Alley towards the Central Bank plaza.

'I guess I should be going too,' I said, but made no move to leave.

'Me too,' she said.

'Can I walk you to a cab?' I offered.

'Why don't we go for a pint?' she said.

'Oh I don't know,' I said without thinking, and was on the point of correcting myself and saying *Christ, yes, of course yes*, when I saw a look of disappointment crest on her face, and then subside, which made me glad that I had hesitated; it made me feel that my hopes were not entirely forlorn, so I told her, 'Ah go on then. A nightcap. I could do with one.'

At her suggestion we went to Gogarty's, just down the street. A couple were leaving as we arrived and we squeezed into the seats they had vacated, sitting side by side. There was no table between us now. Dee was wearing a grey skirt-suit, set off by a round-necked white top and black tights. I let my eyes drop every now and then, when I thought I wouldn't be detected, to her legs—those parts, that is, that were exposed: the skirt riding up, the flesh pushed out to both sides where they took her weight on the chair, but pulled sheer on top, so that I could see the little stubs of hair on her thighs poking through.

Several awkward attempts at conversation were initiated

and then abandoned, and I feared that it was going to be one of those excruciating encounters you have with people you have nothing in common with except that you work together, and was lining up excuses to leave after the first drink, when something clicked and we began to converse with ease.

'Serve Larry right if he got bitten,' she said at one point, 'going fishing for sharks. I didn't even know we had sharks in Ireland.'

'Not "in Ireland", Dee,' I corrected, ' "in Irish waters". If they were *in* Ireland, we'd all be in trouble.'

'Don't get all pedantic on me, Mr Writer,' she said, laying her hand briefly on mine. 'You want another pint?'

'Sure,' I said.

I watched her move through the crowd to the bar. I thought back to my first day in Aisling, when I had walked behind her up the stairs. I may earlier have reported what I saw then in strictly factual terms, but whatever I may have seen, what I reacted to was the way in which her trousers had stretched tautly across her buttocks. I had wanted Dee, that first day, but only in the abstract way all straight men are condemned to want most every woman they meet, even if it's only entertaining an idea, placing them into categories according to their desirability and your degree of desperation. And I wanted her now, as she pressed back to the table with our pints, a smile on her face. But the want was not now in any way abstract.

'Cheers,' she said, holding up her glass for me to tap.

'*Sláinte,*' I said, clinking my glass against hers. I dismissed again as absurd the idea that anything would happen between us. Absurd, yes: patently absurd. It was in fact something (one of the few things) on which Tom and I had agreed.

When he'd still been with Aisling, he and I and Dee had

once had a meeting together, during which he had noticed the way my eyes had tracked her as she'd left to go to the little girls' room.

'Caught you,' he said.

'What?' I said, untangling my eyes and bringing them back to the table.

'Oh come on, you were totally checking out Deirdre's arse.'

'Wasn't.'

'Eoin ...'

'Maybe a little,' I conceded, blushing.

'Don't feel bad about it,' he said, 'men look at women all the time. Where you fancy, let your eyes follow. That's what they were designed for. Just don't get your hopes up.'

'What do you mean?' I asked.

'Just that she's well out of your league, mate.'

'She's fucking well out of yours too,' I snapped.

'Do you think so?'

'Definitely,' I said.

'Maybe. She's not really my type anyway. She's a bit too Rubenesque for me.'

'Rubenesque?'

'I believe the polite term is "big boned". I'm more of a "Warrior Princess" man myself.'

'What the fuck are you talking about?'

'Something I came up with a while ago; a way of categorising women. Tom's Typology of Totty, I call it.'

I laughed, and my irritation at him passed. 'Typology of Totty?'

'Do you want to hear it?'

'Dee will be back soon.'

'I'll write it up and email it to you then.'

'That's OK,' I said, 'just tell me what you mean by "Rubenesque" and "Warrior Princess"?'

'Well, to understand that you have to understand that nature has designed just nine basic female body types, which are, in the order they appeared in the species: Stone Age Woman, Warrior Princess, Venusian, Rubenesque, Everywoman, Pretty Girl, Beauty Queen, Supermodel and Waif.'

'OK.'

'They're not very imaginative names, I know, but they do conjure up certain mental pictures, don't they?'

'I'm not a very visual person.'

'Well, take "Stone Age Woman", for instance. What does that name conjure up, conceptually? Most people would see a tough, plain, hardy woman, and they'd see right, because you needed to be tough back then: you had to bear your children, gather the berries and the other wild fruit, fend off attacks by wild animals.'

'Do you give examples?'

'I just gave you an example.'

'I mean examples of real people.'

'I could probably come up with something if I gave it some thought.'

'Do that. Because if I knew what you were looking for I could maybe set you up with someone; or put an ad on a lonely hearts website for you: "Dashing Prince of Programming seeks Warrior Woman to assimilate". What do you think?'

'I think you'd be wasting your time,' he sniffed, sensing correctly that his classification was being mocked. 'I'm not into that whole relationship thing. It's a fucking charade.'

'Spread yourself around?'

'I don't spread myself at all,' he replied. 'I'm exploring celibacy at the moment.'

'But don't you miss ...?'

'Miss what?' he pre-empted.

'You know ... companionship?'

'You mean sex?'

'Not only sex.'

'It's only ever about sex, really,' he answered wearily. 'And you? You anyone's companion at the moment?'

He put a snide inflection on the word *companion* and I followed the implication by saying, 'No, I'm nobody's companion at the moment.'

I had hoped that Tom would conclude from my response that there had been no one since Erin, and there hadn't been, in the sense that I had had no relationships since the break-up, yet there had been 'assignations', as it were, post-nightclub couplings from which I had derived no satisfaction—punctuated as they had all been by the frantic flatulent noises made by two bodies slapping together more out of instinct than desire—but in which I had engaged for months, for more than a year, after the break-up.

These encounters continued even after I joined Aisling, though I stopped—just stopped, made a resolution and that was that—one night after I stayed back with Deirdre and the rest of the Comms Team to finalise a proposal that was due to be submitted to the Board the following day. Tom was there too, doing whatever it was he did (I never actually quite fathomed it—'I'm a floater,' he would say, explaining nothing); he suggested we turn on the radio and, when we concurred, he tuned into a late-night talk show on one of the Dublin stations. We came to the programme in the middle of an interview with a doctor from the Family Planning Clinic, who was commenting on the increase of the number of cases of STDs in the city. She was followed by a male caller who claimed to have slept with nearly a hundred different women in the previous six months without contracting an STD.

'In the past six months?' asked the host. 'A hundred women?'

'Give or take,' said the caller.

That stirred something: for the next half-hour we listened to call after call from men and women detailing the number and temporal spread of their sexual partners. One woman claimed to have slept with four hundred men in one year, which shocked even the host.

'I have to say, caller,' he said, 'that I'm not sure I believe you. That's more than one a day.'

'I don't care what ye believe. What I'm telling ye is true.'

You could tell that everyone on the floor had stopped working to listen to the exchange.

'Do you have sex every day?'

'Most days.'

'And is it always with a different man?'

'Yeah.'

'Can I ask why you never sleep with the same man twice?'

'I don't know.'

'You don't know. Do you ever feel ashamed of your behaviour?'

'Why should I feel ashamed? Do ye think I'm doing something wrong?'

'Well,' said the host, carefully, 'I do think that there are aspects of your behaviour you might want to look at. Where do you meet these men?'

'Pubs, discos: the usual places.'

'Do you drink?'

'Yeah, I drink.'

'Do you drink much? I mean, are you drunk when you have sex with these men?'

'Sometimes,' she said.

'Sometimes,' repeated the host. 'Do you use protection?'

'I'm on the Pill, amn't I?'

'The Pill doesn't protect you against STDs. Have you ever had a sexually transmitted disease?'

'No.'

'Have you ever been tested?'

'I told ye that I don't have one of them STDs. I don't need some doctor poking me in the fanny to tell me that.'

'Tell me,' said the host, 'are you not tired of sex?'

There was silence on the line.

'Let me put it another way. Do you really like sex so much that you have to do it every day, sometimes twice a day, with a completely different man?'

'I suppose so.'

'You suppose so? Tell me, do your genitals ever get a little sore?'

'Ouch!' said Emer, from her cubicle. 'What a question to ask.'

'He should ask her if she has a boyfriend,' said Tom from his booth.

'Have you ever had a steady boyfriend?' asked the host.

'I have a boyfriend now,' she said.

'And what's sex like with him?'

'Jesus, Tom,' said Emer, 'you should be on that show.'

'It was an obvious question to ask.'

'Shush,' said Aoife, 'I want to hear what she says.'

'And on that note we'll take a break,' said the host.

'Shit,' said Aoife. 'I missed that.'

'I wonder does her boyfriend know?' asked Emer.

'Well, she's never had sex with him,' I said.

'What?' asked Aoife.

'That's what she claims,' I said: 'she's not going to have sex with him until they get married.'

'He must be some fucking eejit,' said Emer. 'Does he not ask where she goes every night?'

'Forget the boyfriend,' said Tom, 'I want to know if the prostitutes know.'

'Why should they care?' I asked.

'Because it violates the whole principle of commodity exchange,' he said: 'She's giving away for free what men pay good money for. She's probably undermining the whole basis of the sex economy up around Fitzwilliam Square.'

'You should ring in and say that,' suggested Emer.

'I think I will,' he said. I heard him picking up his phone's receiver. I stood up to watch. Aoife and Emer stood up too.

'Tom!' said Dee.

'Relax, Deirdre,' he said, dialling a number. 'I won't mention where I'm working, and if anyone asks, I was on a break. I probably won't get through, anyway—hang on, it's ringing. Hello? Yes, hello, I'm calling about that girl ... yes, my name is Tom, Tom Drover. Great, thank you.' He placed his hand over the receiver. 'I'm in the queue. I can hear the ads on the other end of the line.'

'Right,' said the host, when the ads had finished, 'we've had an overwhelming response to our last caller, so I'm going to go straight to the phones. Let's see—who's on line three?'

'Tom,' said Tom, and a moment later his voice came out of our radio: *Tom.*

'What do you have to say about our last caller?'

'Actually, I'm more interested in saying something to the city's prostitutes.'

'And what would that be?'

'Well, she's giving away for free what they charge good money for. They should have a word with her.'

'That's well out of order, Tom. You're off the air. Next caller!'

'Crash and burn,' said Emer.

'Tell me that you all weren't thinking the same thing.'

'What's your name, caller?'

'I wasn't,' said Dee.

'Sam.'

Tom gave an exaggerated sigh, and said, 'A prophet is never appreciated in his own country.'

'And what do you think of our last caller's behaviour, Sam?'

'I think she's lying.'

'Hear, hear,' I said.

'You think she was lying?' asked Tom.

'Come on,' I said, 'of course she was lying. No one behaves like that. No one is having that much sex.'

'You'd be surprised,' said Tom, leaning on the partition that divided his cubicle from mine. 'Ask a gay man, for instance, how many partners he's had in a year, and four hundred might seem like a severe case of underachievement.'

'That's different,' I said.

'No, it's not,' said Tom, 'except that straight people are more hypocritical about it.'

'Hypocritical or not, how could you do that to yourself?'

'You say that as if sex was something bad.'

'Not bad, but I do think she might have self-esteem issues.'

'Maybe she just knows how to have a good time.'

'Boys, boys,' said Dee, 'that's enough. Time to settle down.

Eoin, you have work to do. And, Tom, stop distracting my team.'

'Sure, Dee,' he said, sitting down. Aoife and Emer had already, with leporine quickness, disappeared from view. I remained standing for a moment, then I too sat down.

*

I suppose that what Tom had meant when he'd classified Dee as 'Rubenesque' was that she did not possess a conventionally pretty physique, and that was true, to a point—but she had what Tom had not mentioned, something he had obviously not factored into his system: *energy*.

I could feel it emanating from her. Or perhaps what I was feeling emanated from within myself and was being projected onto her: my excitement, my anticipation. Wherever it came from—from her, from me, from some fusion of the two—it filled me with longing: I wanted to touch her, and would have if she had given any sign. I would have sat there all night, waiting. But after only a few drinks, Dee had a coughing attack as a result of downing a shot of tequila too quickly, and decided that she'd had enough; time to go home.

'Aisling's not doing so well, Eoin,' she said absently, after I offered to escort her to a taxi rank and put her into a cab. 'The investors are losing confidence.'

I made some absurd joke about the relationship between investors and confidence tricksters. She looked at me blankly. She did not grin, but nor did she grimace. She hadn't heard; or maybe she had heard, but had not understood. She was drunk. Dee was drunk.

I helped her into her coat, held the door open as we stepped out onto Anglesea Street and then felt her slide her arm through mine as we faltered up the cobblestones towards Dame Street and the taxi rank at College Green. There was no physical contact—skin did not touch skin—but it was still too much intimacy; it held out too much hope. I tried to distract myself from her presence by looking for the moon, but couldn't see it—I can't recall now whether that was because the moon was new, or because it had already set, or because it was hidden by cloud.

When we reached the rank there was a long queue and no taxis; we took our place at the back of the line. It was cold for a night in late July, first intimations of autumn. A wind blowing off the Irish Sea scuttled under our jackets and slid through skin and muscle and fat to slice our bones. Dee nuzzled her body next to mine and laid her head on my shoulder. She said something that I didn't catch.

'Sorry?' I said, leaning forward so that I might hear her better, but not enough that I would dislodge her head from its resting place.

'Nothing,' she said, 'nothing.' Her body swayed and she nearly lost her footing. I tied my arm around her waist to help her stabilise herself.

'Tell me,' I insisted. 'What were you going to say?'

'Can't remember.'

'Was it about Aisling, Dee? Was it about the company?'

'Could have been ...'

A taxi arrived and drew in a party of three. The line shuffled forward.

'How's the company doing, Dee? Really?'

'Could be better,' she admitted flatly, and sighed, blowing out a long plume of cloudy air that was lofted up and kited away by the breeze. 'We don't have enough clients, and the ones we do have are not happy with us. I shouldn't be telling you this. You won't tell anyone, will you?'

'Cross my heart,' I said, making the motion above my chest.

The line shuffled forward as two more taxis arrived. Dee didn't say anything else. I could feel the rise and fall of her chest. Her breathing had slowed; she might have been dozing, so I tuned in to what was going on around us. Us. I suppose it must have seemed to other people that we were a couple. It would have been a reasonable assumption given the evidence of their senses. And I too could easily have let myself believe that this was a soberly chosen intimacy, and not an inebriated selection. But she had a boyfriend. Mark. I'd met him once, at the Aisling Christmas party; he worked as a senior database engineer for a big American multinational, though what he really wanted to do was travel.

'Dee has no interest in travel,' he remarked. 'Very focused on her career. Very loyal to Aisling.'

'Why don't you go on your own?' I asked.

'Couldn't do that,' he said. 'Couldn't leave Dee here by herself.'

'Hey,' Dee said, as she came up and put her arm around his waist. 'What are you guys talking about?'

'Nothing, really,' he said.

'Travel,' I said, realising only when he caught my eyes with a reproachful look that it might have been an imprudent thing to say.

'Eoin was telling me about his trip to the States,' he explained to Dee. 'That's all.'

'Plenty of time for travelling after we've made our hay,' she said.

'I know,' he replied but then they looked away from each

other and she withdrew her arm. I mouthed my apologies to him, but he just shrugged his shoulders: *Old story*.

The line moved along again. Dee and I were at the head of it now. The scent and softness of almost her entire weight pressed against me now and her warm, sour breath trickled over the skin of my neck. I experienced a moment of dislocation, as if there were suddenly two consciousnesses overlapping in my body, and neither of them at rest. It felt, indeed, as if both were lurching toward and then away from each other, generating a sensation a bit like vertigo, or maybe motion sickness.

I was obviously a little drunk myself.

I feared I might let Dee drop but then a taxi, thank God, was sluiced from the lights at Church Lane and pulled up at the rank. Ours.

'Where to?' asked the driver when we got into the backseat.

'Rathmines, first,' I said, and realised that, yes, that was as far as this fantasy would go. Rathmines first, and then home for me: everything she had done meant nothing; it certainly meant less that I had read into it, just a woman in a state of inebriation looking for someone solid to lean against, not much more than that.

But I laid my hand on her thigh, and she did not remove it. The fabric of her tights felt like a thin layer of static between her flesh and mine. My heart began to pump blood with quick, urgent expectancy. My penis hardened, and I shifted in my seat, trying to coax it out of the painful position into which it was extending itself but no joy, and I couldn't just put my hand down my pants, that would be too obvious. Could only hope it subsided.

But it didn't, and as the taxi approached Rathmines I felt the weight of an enormous regret press down upon me, and a revulsion at what I was planning to do overcame me. Yet I did not remove my hand from her thigh, nor did my erection abate. My one hope was that when we arrived at her house the lights would be on, meaning that her boyfriend was home and she'd say goodbye, and I would tell the driver to continue on to my apartment, and we'd never say anything more about it—it would be as if it never happened, forgotten.

But there were no lights on when the taxi pulled up at her house. I got out first and offered her my hand. Didn't say anything; didn't make any moves; left it entirely to her.

'Would you like to come in for something to drink?' she said.

'Sure,' I replied, and paid the taxi driver while she walked to the front door. A security light snapped on, and a brilliant white brightness bleached the porch away to nothing. Blinded, I groped my way through the open door into the hallway. Heat, and softer light. She had turned on the lamp that rested on a waist-high telephone table beside the door. Black and white photographs hung on the magnolia walls. The carpet was red.

'Let's go into the kitchen,' she said, walking towards a door at the end of the corridor.

I can't do this. I should go. I should just turn and go.

She opened the door and I followed her into a room divided in two by a breakfast bar. A small round table was positioned in the foreground. Behind the bar was the kitchen proper: cooker with gas hobs, fan oven, large silver fridge, worktops, wine rack, espresso machine, utensils, utilities.

I catalogued all these things to distract myself.

Don't look. Don't look at her.

'Would you like tea or coffee?' she asked, 'or something stronger?' She stood with her back to me. I stepped up behind her and slid my arms around her waist. She did not resist.

Resist!

I kissed the back of her neck, tasting her sweat, alcohol-infused, and overlain by deposits of cigarette smoke and the lingering after-effects of her perfume. She did not push me away. She sighed.

Push me away!

She turned and offered her mouth to be kissed, which I did, encountering her tongue and the tang of her breath, like sweet burnt herbs.

Then we—look, let's stop being coy. You want the juicy details? Here are the juicy details:

We're in the bedroom. I am lying on the bed, which is unmade. Dee has excused herself and dashed into the en suite bathroom. There are two lockers, but one is empty of artefacts. I notice this, even though I am in the grip of an almost unbearable excitement. My prick throbs in time with the bruising, timpanning, arrhythmic clatter of my heart, which is reverberating in every vein in my body: down my legs, in my stomach, at the back of my neck, across my scalp. My throat is dry. My palms are moist.

When Dee returns from the bathroom, she is wearing only a bra and a pair of panties. She crosses the room and clambers on top of me. I am still wearing all my clothes, having not even taken off my jacket. She leans down and unbuckles my belt, and makes to pull off my trousers. I lift my bum and she slides them down to my ankles; I kick them off. They land on the far side of the room. She laughs, resumes her seat on me and leans forward. We kiss. My turn. I slip my hands up her back and attempt to unclasp her bra but I clumsily snap it hard against her skin and she winces. Shrugging off my efforts she sits back and reaches behind to unclip it herself. Her stomach creases with the exertion. I look at her face, but can't see her eyes: they are closed, concentrating. Her hands drop to her side. She hunches her shoulders, and rolls them forward; the straps of her bra slacken and slither down her upper arms. She lets them slither, and smiles at me, but I don't smile back: I am looking at her breasts. Encased in their cups they had seemed the most magnificent and mysterious glands but, unconstrained, they have lost their suggestive curves, flopping forward instead to triangular tips, distinguished by two large cherry-blossom pink aureoles on which nipples have yet to discriminate themselves.

They are not as fantastic as I had imagined, but they are more real, and more beautiful. Laughing, I reach up to stroke them.

She cocks her head. 'What's funny?' Dangerous undertone.

'Nothing,' I say. 'Nothing at all.' The excitement centred on my genitals is dissipating. The energy, having no outlet, is seeping back into the organism that generated it, diffusing into every cell, every organ: from my toes to the follicles on my scalp, I feel a delicate, tingling sensation, as if my body is being gently rubbed. Every nerve feels alive, equally alive, none are prioritised. The feel of the sheets on which I lie is as important, as illuminating, as significant, as the solidity of Dee's body on my groin and hips. But even these sensations pass. My body is in fact emptied of sensations. My mind is still. No chattering, no stories: just a poised awareness. It's like. It's like. What is it like? It is like the moment between climax and orgasm but infinitely extended. Yes. And oh I could exist like this forever, but I know that I cannot. This has happened to me before—once before—and I know what's coming. And it comes: a huge liquid sense of compassion gushes up from my heart and floods me with an impartial love for everyone and everything, with all their flaws and imperfections and weaknesses, which are not after all flaws and imperfections and weaknesses inherent to them but interpretations of their behaviour arising out of my own limited understanding because I realise now that everyone, everything, is already perfect, and to perfect yourself you do not need to act, you do not need to pray or meditate or fast: all you need to do is perceive this perfection.

Which is not so easy when the illuminated moment has passed, passed back into the everyday; not so easy to habitually perceive the world in this way, every moment during the dichotomies of daily life.

Dee's hand has rolled down the elastic band of my boxers and is massaging my flaccid penis. I place my hand on her wrist.

'Nothing's going to happen,' I say.

'Is something wrong?'

'Nothing's wrong. I just can't do this.'

'I want to do this,' she says.

My member twitches at her frank expression of desire for me, but no, no, and I say so: 'It wouldn't be right.'

'Right for who?'

'Dee,' I insist, 'it wouldn't be right. And anyway, we're colleagues; what would Larry say?'

She shakes off the loose grip of my hand and rolls off me onto the other side of the bed. 'I don't give a fuck what Larry would say,' she says. 'You should go.'

'Of course.' I stand up, and hobble across the room to retrieve my trousers. 'Listen,' I say, as I put them on again, 'have a good weekend, OK? I'll see you on Tuesday.'

She does not respond, and I can feel my moment of illumination fast fading away. Fuck.

I find myself about to say, snidely, 'Suit yourself,' but I check myself, breathe deeply. I stop at the door.

'Well bye then,' I say, hoping it sounds like, *No hard feelings, nothing personal.*

I turn to go.

'Larry has his suspicions about you, you know.'

'What?'

'He thinks it's a bit of a coincidence you being a flatmate of Fergus's *and* a friend of the man who set up that bloody website.'

She has rolled onto her side to face me, her head propped up on an elbow. She has not covered herself.

'That investigator,' she says, noting my surprised expression, 'did a profile of every member of staff. The things we found out. You set off a lot of alarms.'

My gorge rises. The back of my throat is coated with the acrid foretaste of sick. It is only by screwing shut my jaws that I stop myself from vomiting.

I should not be hearing this from Dee.

'But I defended you,' she continues. She drops onto her back. 'I said you were loyal.'

'I am loyal.'

She only laughs.

'Dee, you have to believe me.'

'That was the end of Larry and me,' she says. 'I think he was tired of hearing me defend you. "Let's take a break," he said, "until this whole thing settles down." '

'Dee—'

'If it was you, you know, I'll never forgive you.'

Why did she have to say these things? The feeling of illumination has gone completely now, and in its place another has arisen: hate—as if, because I had been filled with love (and I mean real love, not just desire or lust; mystical upper-case-L Love: unequivocal, unconditional, universal), and then so quickly emptied of it, I was susceptible to possession by love's opposite.

No, that's not it, not precisely. I expect it's more that the normal state of man (of humans, I mean; let's be egalitarian about this) is hate, and that when we are filled up with love, however briefly, we afterwards can become more conscious— no, not even 'more conscious', just simply *conscious* of the amount of hate we have within ourselves.

I had been spared from it for an hour, less than an hour, mere minutes, even if the interlude had seemed longer. And I'm grateful for that, however short it was, but I still left Dee's place not only intensely aware of the hate I harboured but also focused. Resolved.

And, well, you know the rest. You know what happens next. You know what I was driven to do on the *Maeldun*.

Still. You want an explanation. You feel it's the least you deserve—especially as you're thinking that Larry did nothing to me that adds up to a motive for murder; not in his actions or inactions; not even in his hypocrisy—and I would dearly love to oblige, but I can't.

No, that's not right, I can oblige. There is actually an explanation—it's just that it wasn't any one thing in particular; it wasn't even anything that Larry did or failed to do; really, in the end, it had more to do with the fact that ever since I lost my childhood religion (and I did lose it, I set it aside one day as I might have set aside a toy that I had outgrown, and when I returned years later to look for it out of a sense of nostalgia I could not recall where I had placed it, nor how I might recover it) I have been searching for an alternative, something to believe in that would not only satisfy my need for the numinous but would also not make too many demands on my credulity. The problem, right there. No belief would place such a high premium on faith if it were not so difficult to attain—and sustain. And yet, the reward: to know, to know with certainty that one will be saved, that one is a member of the chosen people, that everything has a purpose.

I now believe that I'm temperamentally unsuited for believing in anything. That's OK. Not everyone is equipped to believe. There are those who create belief, the progenitors, Christ and Buddha and Shankara and Mohammed, mystical geniuses, the religious virtuosi; those who preserve a faith, the masses and their guides, the priests and imams and monks of this world; and those who destroy belief, the infidels, the Judases. Tom had left Aisling because he did not believe in it, not the way Larry wanted, and he was determined to create something for himself. I could not hope to accomplish such a thing. I was simply not coded for such an endeavour. I was coded, on the contrary, for destruction, and when I could not destroy Aisling (however vainly I tried), I was bound to destroy Larry.

Bound to: yes. Nature acts. All thoughts and emotions, both munificent and murderous, arise in Her: the body passively reacts according to its biological programming, and the Self—the true Self, that is—observes, content to let the divine plot unfold, having faith that the Author (if there is an Author) will have skill enough to resolve all loose ends and inconsistencies by story's end.

I did what I did because I did what I did. In the end, this is the only explanation that any of us can ever truly sign up to.

It's the only explanation you're going to get.

Case Study VI

(Source: various Irish recruitment websites)

Responding Flexibly to New Challenges

Communications Executive
(Temporary/Contract)

The Role

Our client, a Dublin-based IT consultancy, is seeking to recruit a Communications Executive to assist its Marketing Manager in servicing the company's communications needs.

The vacancy has arisen as a result of a re-branding process and the successful candidate will take responsibility, under the direction of the Marketing Manager, for updating the company's suite of external and internal literature—including its website, corporate brochure, intranet, etc.—to reflect the company's new brand ethos.

The successful candidate will also be expected to take responsibility for the ongoing maintenance of the company's website, and to assist the Marketing Manager in responding to any communications issues that may arise on a day-to-day basis.

Requirements

The ideal candidate will possess a degree in business or computing, with a Master's in Journalism. However, our client will also accept applications from candidates with a degree in communications or journalism and relevant experience in the business and/or computing fields.

The ideal candidate will also possess excellent writing skills, be self-motivated and energetic, and demonstrate an ability to work as a part of a team.

Experience

At least two years' experience in a similar role.

Conditions

Commercial hours, including evenings and some weekends. As our client also has offices in the US, some travel may also be involved.

Package

Negotiable salary, commensurate with experience.

Position

Temporary, 12-month contract.

Contact Information

Send your CV, together with a covering letter and three short writing samples, to patricia.cadigan@binneach-recruiting.ie.

7. Prospects: Aisling's Future Plans

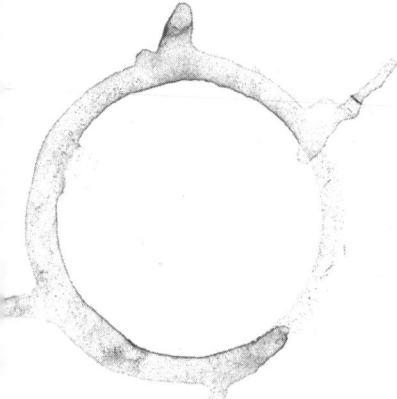

So this, I suppose, is story's end, for Aisling at least; though, yes, you're right, there are still one or two loose ends to clear up.

Such as, what exactly happened to you after you got back from the fishing expedition?

What happened was this: the following Saturday I was going down Grafton Street when I spotted Tom walking towards me. At first I thought (and hoped) that he would be swept by without noticing me, and that I'd be able to just walk on without having to talk to him but, no, he saw me and raised his hand in greeting.

We moved towards each other. He asked me how things were. I told him that things were fine.

'Arrah, go way,' he said. 'I heard what happened.'

'Could be worse,' I said.

He raised a sceptical eyebrow, but didn't press the point; he asked instead if I was hungry and, when I said that I was, suggested that we go to the National Gallery for a bite to eat.

'Sounds great,' I said, though I wondered what his agenda was: I had often proposed the Gallery as a place where we might have one of our lunches together, and he had always vetoed the idea. I sensed that we had resumed our old rivalry, and so, after we had purchased our meals from the buffet and found a table, I decided to make a counter feint by telling him about Larry and Dee, being casual with the information, but still letting it sound like the revelation it was.

He said, 'You're telling me this like it was big news.'

'Isn't it?'

'It was going on for ages,' he said. 'Are you only after finding out about it now?'

I nodded.

'Jesus, I can't believe you didn't know that Larry was shagging Dee.' He laughed but something far from affable glinted in his eyes.

'How long have you known?'

'Since almost as soon as I joined Aisling. It was fairly fucking obvious.'

'Not to me it wasn't.'

'It was Aisling's great open secret,' he said, 'everyone knew about it.'

'I never bloody did.'

'Christ, almighty, Cullen,' he declared, 'if you don't stop

whining and start paying attention to what's going on, life is going to keep kicking the crap out of you.'

'Well how come you never mentioned it to me?' I asked.

'Because I assumed that you had a pair of fucking eyes.'

I couldn't look at him. I pushed the crumbs around on my otherwise barren plate.

'Let's walk,' he said.

We passed through the rooms on the ground floor of the original building. Tom did most of the talking, just as he always had (and, indeed, in its outward particulars, the encounter was holding fast to the pattern of our previous lunches, as if we had last seen each other only the day before and not months ago, after an awkward parting). The latest piece of news, he told me as we moved into a new space in the long gallery of Irish painting, was that he was changing the name of his company.

'We're UCON now,' he said. 'U-C-O-N, all caps. Apparently it's the original Native American spelling of the word.'

'Is it really?'

'Ah of course not, but it'll sound good in the brochure. Actually, it's meant to suggest both the phrase "You can" and the word "Icon", so it ties in with our IT skillset and signifies our can-do and empowering attitude towards our work.' He grinned, and had the grace to do it deprecatingly; he sounded like a man who had formerly eschewed all interest in the specifics of home furnishings, only to find himself, after buying a house, discussing with enthusiasm the relative merits of carpets versus wooden floors, curtains versus blinds. 'We paid a branding company in London a fucking fortune to come up with it.'

'You don't seem too gone on it.'

'I'm not, really, but Basking loves it.'

'Why would Basking care?' I asked, although I had a dreadful apprehension. Tom touched a finger to his nose.

'Tom,' I demanded: 'Tell me.'

He cocked his head to the left and looked at me, one eye higher than the other. 'Who do you think is bankrolling the company?' he asked, then clicked his head back to its normal level.

'Some venture-capital firm, I presumed.'

'And you presumed correctly,' he said, 'only it's a venture-capital firm that happens to be run by Basking'—of course, I thought, of fucking course—'and Maeve Muckian. You remember her?'

'Never met her,' I said. We had stopped in front of a large painting of a young woman standing in contemplation beside a river. I leaned forward to read the information tag, then straightened up. 'I don't know how you can take that man's money, especially after what he did to you.'

'Oh get over yourself, will you?' he said. His arms were folded, and his head was tilted again, appraising the picture. 'He never did anything to me, nothing serious. He thought I was just another Larry-clone, that's all, and when he realised that I wasn't—'

'What about the Ninth Wave deal? I know he put his name to the proposal that tore your submission to pieces.'

'It was a message. He wanted me to move out of consultancy, which I was only doing to piss Larry off, even though frankly I wasn't much good at it. So Ninth Wave was good, a wakeup call. We're into product development now. We're creating a web-based, personalised micro-marketing solution. It's much healthier.'

We stood, silent, for a few moments.

'What do you think of this?'

'It's nice,' I said, though I had hardly examined it. I looked at the information tag again: *Revêrie (Dreaming), 1882*. 'You?'

'I think it's fucking awful: the autumnal palette, the way it's all slightly out of focus, the idealised peasant girl. Typical Celtic Mist shite.'

I considered the canvas again.

'You seem to know what you like,' I said.

'I know what I don't like.'

'Maybe you should retire and become a painter yourself,' I teased.

'I think I probably will,' he said. 'Eventually.'

I glanced at him.

'I'm not going to be doing this forever,' he explained.

'Doing what?'

'Working. I plan to make my fortune and retire by the time I'm thirty-five. Forty, tops.'

'To paint?'

'Among other things.'

I gave a laugh. It sounded louder than I had intended, and cracked the careful hush of the room; the three or four other patrons in there with us, as well as the guard, cast disapproving looks in our direction.

Tom didn't seem to notice. Or care. 'You don't believe me?' he asked.

'I believe you,' I said quietly.

'You don't think I'm serious.'

'I think you're deadly serious,' I said. 'But why not do it now? Why not just retire to some cottage down the country and start painting now?'

'Because I'm enjoying myself at the moment. Besides, art is for the middle-aged. No one has anything to say before they turn forty, nothing worth hearing.'

'Tom,' I said, preparing to ask him the question I had wanted to put to him since we'd met, but he interrupted me:

'You want a job.'

I couldn't tell from his manner whether he was seeking clarification (*You want a job?*) or had simply finished my sentence for me. I swallowed, the wet undulating pop of my Adam's apple sounding unfeasibly distinct. I wanted to respond with something smart and non-committal like, 'If you think that would fit in with your plans,' or, 'If you think you could use my skills,' but what I said was, simply, 'Yes.'

'I don't know,' he said. 'I mean, we are looking for someone to work on our literature, but I don't think you'd be UCON material.'

I didn't push it. I hadn't rated my chances, anyway, since learning that Basking was financing the operation.

'You're really not suited for this sort of thing, Eoin.' He must have realised that this had cut, because he went on quickly, in a soothing tone, 'It's nothing personal. It's just an observation. And it's for your own good. You're just not cut out to be a Celtic Cub.'

I tried not to obviously react.

'It's a personality thing.'

'Personality,' I repeated.

'Someone once told me,' he said, as if a jocular aside would pacify me, 'that although there are at least sixteen different personality profiles, Irish banks only give permanent positions to people with one of two types.'

'Just two?'

'Yep, just two: those who have absolutely no scruples and those who're willing to follow without question the orders of those with absolutely no scruples.' He snorted. 'But I didn't say that, if anyone asks ...'

'That's awful,' I said.

'I think it's a fucking brilliant idea. Firms should be free to hire whoever the hell they want.' His excited voice echoed in the room. More disapproving looks were directed at us.

'What about those people who don't have the right personalities?' I asked and although I wanted to sound angry, even righteous, I barely managed to raise more than a whisper.

He barked a bitter little yelp of a laugh. 'That's what the service industries were invented for.' He soaked up my look of appalled censure. 'You want fries with that?' he added in a mock-American drawl.

I laughed. Uneasily. In absolute terms, it was not the worst or most pejorative thing that Tom had ever said to me. But the tone. Perhaps it was the tone he had always used with me; perhaps I had never truly heard it before (had perhaps never truly wanted to hear it), only to hear it now and to realise that Tom sounded different than I had ever supposed.

Larry had been a big one for listening. 'As much as we need to speak our truths,' he'd said, 'we need to also listen to the truths that others are speaking, because normally we don't listen, we merely project our prejudices onto those we interact with, hearing only what is comfortable for our egos to heed.

'To hear someone, to really hear them,' he'd gone on, 'can be a profoundly distressing experience.'

Standing there beside Tom, in a sudden asphyxiating silence, after hearing for the first time, really hearing, what he thought of me, I understood what Larry had meant, finally hearing him too.

*

Larry's not dead, you know. Oh go on, of course you know. Don't tell me that you actually thought he was dead. That I had it in me to kill him. That all along I was telling you the whole truth and nothing but, et cetera, et cetera. You did? Really?

Well.

If it means anything, I didn't deliberately set out to deceive you. It just sort of came out that way. I suppose, looking back over what I have written, that it was wishing thinking on my behalf, wishful thinking in the way that Larry talks about it. *If you believe in something strongly enough,* he would say, *the universe will see to it that you get what you deserve.* And I suppose, too, that I was trying to pass off some of the burden of that belief onto you. I must have hoped that if enough people assumed he was dead then in some sense (some symbolic sense) he would be dead.

Because clearly I didn't have enough conviction for the universe to come through for me on my own account. Back on the boat (that much is true, there was a shark-fishing trip) I had watched his spine bend and arch as he struggled with the shark; had visualised myself placing my hands on his back and exerting forward pressure; had pictured him being consumed in the water—had even imagined that it was my karma (my karma!) to do this.

Yet I couldn't do it. I couldn't get my body to follow through on my mind's desires. Paralysed, but unwilling to let my just chance slip away, I prayed desperately for the universe to send a freak wave that would catch Larry and toss him overboard without my having to do anything. But no. The sea hardly wavered. Larry remained stubbornly alive. It seemed that I lacked even a heretic's faith.

And I think that Larry knew, knew that I had at least entertained the idea, because after the shark had been gaffed onto the deck, weighed, photographed and released, he had directed at me a keen, speculative look and had then declined to talk to me during the return to shore or during the long drive back to Dublin. When I arrived in the office at nine the following Tuesday, I was told by Sheila that Larry was in the boardroom and wanted to have a word with me, ASAP. When I got there, I found him sitting at the head of the table with Aengus and Basking on either side of him. After having misread the portents so often with Dee, I was in no doubt as to what was intended. Larry said nothing. He left it to Basking to invite me to have a seat and to then explain that during a standard personnel review it had been noted that my performance had not met a certain standard.

'Not to mention the fact,' he said, 'that we also think you've been shafting the company.'

He said this as casually as he might have dropped a non sequitur about the weather into the conversation (*Not to mention the fact that it hasn't stopped raining in days*), but without averting his rapacious eyes from me or in any way altering his expression. I did my best to simply smile at him in return.

'We can't prove anything, not conclusively,' he continued in the same controlled, almost unconcerned, tone, 'and we understand that your contract says that you can't be fired without good reason, but,' sliding a manila folder towards me, 'there are documents in there that are quite—uh—suggestive, and which, if brought to the attention of the Guards, could get someone in a lot of trouble, so ...'

I flicked through the printouts in the folder. As far as I could manage, I did not allow my expression to change; still smiling, I said, 'That's fine. Time to move on anyway. I've done all I can here.'

Basking said, 'Someone will escort you to your desk, where you can collect your personal effects. Then we'd like you to leave. There's a cheque in there that clears any wages we might owe you.'

'Thanks,' I said. Then, 'Thanks, Aengus,' and, finally, as I stood up, 'Thanks, Larry.'

Aengus didn't look at me, but Larry did. First time he'd looked at me since I'd seated myself. He smiled, but not in any smug or triumphant way; it was in apology, as if in some way he empathised with what I had done, understood the impulse, even if he did not fully approve: it was a smile more of self-reproach than of reproach. I thought he was trying to communicate to me that he was sorry for having caused me to contemplate the things I had contemplated, for having caused me to do the things I had done, the things I had wanted to do.

I wouldn't take my word for that, though.

*

And that was that: the end of my time with Aisling. The end of Aisling, too, at least as I had known it. I heard not long afterwards that Larry had left to become a high-level coach to companies and individual executives; I never discovered if his departure was voluntary or if he had been persuaded to leave. Basking, of course, was promoted to CEO, O'Connor became the General Manager, Essentia were de-hired and the company was quickly repositioned: 'We believe in nothing now,' Basking claimed on the revamped website, 'except getting results.'

Dee left as well, taking Emer and Aoife with her. The three of them now operate a small communications consultancy (Triad Design and Communications) out of an office down in

Ringsend, though I haven't talked to her, or seen her, since our truncated night together.

Tom's doing fine, too, as is UCON. Thriving. From what people tell me. I don't go looking for news of him.

*

But you still have questions. You still want to know some things. Such as: Did you really almost manage to bed Dee? Were you the person who sent the email tipping off the bank about Fergus's code? And did you file the reports that pushed Aisling into b2gb.com's Red Zone?

Basically, you're asking me how much of this you can believe.

To which I respond: you can believe as much or as little of it as you like. No, I mean it. It's fine. Truly. I don't get much of a say, anyway. Once you've paid your cash (or your library dues, for those of you in the nosebleed seats) it stops being my property and passes to you, to do with what you will.

Don't feel bad: I'm glad to be rid of it. I don't even know why I wrote it. After Erin and I broke up, I swore that I'd never write again, but it has been difficult for me to find work since leaving Aisling, and I haven't been able to afford to go travelling, so writing this passed the time I guess. And I started it in hope. I told myself that if I couldn't contain the truth of multitudes in a book I could at least try to contain the truth of my own multitudes but no, no: all I managed to write were lies. Look, I'm not too bothered. Nothing that we say actually means anything—anything real. Anything true. It's all an illusion, an act, the creation of personality through locution: I speak, ergo sum, and the sum of my ego is the tally of all the words I have ever spoken.

So I'm done with words. I have been purged of that ambition. I have another ambition now: to disappear. Literally. I crave dissolution. I crave the bliss I felt with Dee—and felt with Erin, too. Erin? Yes, Erin: I mentioned when I was with Dee (didn't I?) that I had experienced this sensation once before. Well, that once before was with Erin.

'Is something the matter?' she had asked as the energy that had gathered in my genitals began to course back out into the world, erasing as it went any sense of difference between me and it (between *Me*, I should say; between *Us*).

'Shush,' I said, 'shush.' I didn't know what was happening. I should tell you—though I don't know if you'll believe me—that I had prior to this been a virgin and my first thought was that this was an orgasm, but I did not expend much effort grasping after categorisation. All my attention was concentrated upon the sensation; I wanted it with more finesse than I had ever wanted anything; I wanted it without craving it, but:

'Is it me?'

She had been reluctant to disrobe in front of me, her first time too—and she had a thing about her body (fat, she thought), even though I had assured her that I was very much attracted to her ampleness—but her question had re-established an awareness of the boundaries of my self, so, irritated, I lied, saying,

'Yes.'

'And you don't want me?'

'God no,' I said, hateful now. 'Of course not. No.'

Acknowledgments

I could not have completed this novel without the support of a number of people.

I would like, in particular, to thank Marsha Swan, my publisher and editor at Hag's Head Press, whose dogged championing of *Aisling Ltd* has been both inspiring and humbling. She had, in the end, more faith in the book than I, and for that I am profoundly grateful.

My close friend, Kris Surroy, also deserves thanks. By graciously lending me his expertise he saved an entire chapter from being scrapped and rewritten. Thanks, man.

My deepest gratitude, however, is reserved for my partner Pauline. Not only did she keep me sane during the process of writing this book, she also helped me with the research, acting as my principal fact-checker. Her input has immeasurably improved the veracity of the text.

Any mistakes that remain are, needless to say, wholly my responsibility. I should point out, however, that some of these mistakes are deliberate, particularly those that relate to the location, character and environs of 'Kilcoyle House'.

S.D.H., *Athenry, November 2005*

A Note on the Type

The text is set in Veljovic, the first typeface designed by Jovica Veljovic, born in 1954 in Suvi Do, Serbia and Montenegro. Influenced by the German designer Hermann Zapf and Israeli designer Henri Friedlander, he created this crisp type design for the International Typeface Corporation in 1984. His work is also strongly influenced by the fact that he is native to two writing systems: Latin and Cyrillic. His career has encompassed work as a graphic designer, type designer, typographer, calligrapher and teacher. He is now professor of lettering at the Hamburg University of Applied Sciences.

Franklin Gothic, one of the most popular sans serif types ever produced, was designed by Morris Fuller Benton between 1902 and 1912 for the American Type Founders Company. There were already many gothics in America in the early 1900s, but Benton was probably influenced by the popular German grotesks: Basic Commercial and Reform from D. Stempel AG. Early types without serifs were known by the misnomer 'gothic' in America ('grotesque' in Britain and 'grotesk' in Germany). ITC Franklin Gothic, used here for the display headings and emails, is a set of fonts based on Benton's work, re-drawn and expanded on by Victor Caruso in 1980 and David Berlow in 1991.